A SEAL's Honor

ALSO BY JM STEWART

The Military Match Series
A SEAL's Courage
A SEAL's Strength

The Seattle Bachelors Series
Bidding on the Billionaire
Winning the Billionaire
Bargaining for the Billionaire
Claiming the Billionaire

A SEAL's Honor

JM Stewart

FOREVER
YOURS

New York   Boston

Forever Yours
Hachette Book Group
1290 Avenue of the Americas
New York, NY 10104
forever-romance.com
twitter.com/foreverromance

First ebook and print on demand edition: January 2018

Forever Yours is an imprint of Grand Central Publishing. The Forever Yours name and logo are trademarks of Hachette Book Group, Inc.

The publisher is not responsible for websites (or their content) that are not owned by the publisher.

The Hachette Speakers Bureau provides a wide range of authors for speaking events. To find out more, go to www.hachettespeakersbureau.com or call (866) 376-6591.

ISBN 978-1-5387-2886-4 (print on demand edition)
ISBN 978-1-5387-1177-4 (ebook edition)

A SEAL's Honor

A SEAL's Honor

CHAPTER ONE

Of all the places Marcus Denali expected to find himself on the Fourth of July, a singles masquerade ball at the Four Seasons Hotel wasn't one of them.

He poked a finger into his tuxedo collar, trying to loosen the noose as he scanned the ballroom. The entire place looked like the Fourth of July section at Walmart had exploded. Red, white, and blue covered every available surface. Streamers were strung from the ceiling. US flags adorned every table. Hell, they'd even scattered balloons on the floor. To top it off, a live band played on a stage on the far-right end, the music just loud enough to scrape his already shaky nerves.

Gabe, his business partner and one of his best friends, was probably laughing his ass off right about now. For the first time in months, Marcus had a date. An actual date, not his usual weekend excursion, and from a matchmaking service no less. Gabe had met his girlfriend, Steph, through Military Match and had recommended the service. Gabe had gotten lucky, though; the son of a bitch had met Steph in the park for their date. Somewhere neutral that didn't require a damn monkey suit.

Military Match hadn't been cheap, but the woman he'd spoken with had assured him she had the highest standards for her clients. Which was the reason he'd signed up. He needed a girlfriend. Or at least someone who could play the part. A nice girl he could see for a while who'd pass Gram's muster. He hated lying to her. It went against everything she'd ever taught him. But he wanted her to relax and stop worrying about when he was going to get married. Her complaints were always the same. He worked too much. Why wasn't he seeing anybody? When would he finally settle down? The latest argument had started because she'd called him on a Friday night and he was actually home.

Though he had to admit, he'd come tonight because he *wanted* someone to lose himself in for a while. Something a bit more than a one-night stand, but with someone who wouldn't want to tie him down.

So here he was, being strangled by a bow tie, waiting for a date he wouldn't know if she knocked him over. He'd been instructed to meet her at the entrance, but how the hell would he know her? Every woman in the room wore a mask. Was hers dark blue like his? Were the masks identical? Hell. He should've asked, but he hadn't been on an actual date in . . . years.

He straightened off the wall, resisting the urge to undo his tie and the top few buttons of his blasted shirt, and scanned in another direction. Five more minutes. If his date didn't show by then, he was getting the hell out of here.

A small brunette breezed through the doorway, coming to a stop beside him. "Kind of pretentious, huh?"

He ought to turn and greet her. Smile. Introduce himself. Be friendly. He couldn't muster the energy. The whole night set out before him exhausted him. The thought of the fireworks display later set his nerves on edge. Since he'd retired from the SEALs two years ago, he'd always stayed home on the Fourth. Tonight's masquerade was barely a mile from where they'd set the damn things off. He'd definitely need his veterans support group after this. Hell, half the damn room would likely need some sort of therapy after tonight.

He shrugged, aiming for friendly but aloof. "This isn't normally my kind of scene."

"I can tell. You've tugged on your collar four times in the last minute alone."

Marcus finally forced himself to glance at his companion. Her mask caught his attention. Cobalt blue, matching her eyes, with silver lace trim that ran down the right half of her face. Something about those eyes and the dark curls bouncing around her chin nagged at him as being familiar, but with the lights turned low, he couldn't see her well enough to figure out why. Was she the date he'd been waiting for?

She was gorgeous, whoever she was. The heart-shaped neckline of her black dress showed off enough cleavage to tease, filling his head with the luscious fantasy of getting to peel it off her. The sheer, wispy fabric of the skirt floated around shapely thighs he could easily envision wrapped around his hips. Someone like her was exactly what he needed. Cute but wholesome.

He straightened off the wall, tossing her a playful smile as he narrowed his gaze on her. "You've been watching me."

Amusement glinted in her eyes as she tipped her head back to look up at him. "Guilty as charged. I was told to meet my date in this spot, and I wondered if you might be him." She turned back to the room at large, scanning the crowd. "So, what exactly *is* your scene?"

Okay. He'd play her game. For now. He copied her stance and turned to the watch the dancers in front of the stage.

"Somewhere quiet. To be honest, there are too many people in here for my comfort." He jabbed a finger at the flashing ball of death in the ceiling. "And that damn disco ball is giving me a migraine. The funny part is, I used to be the party guy."

At least, he had been before his sister, Ava, died. And before his time in Afghanistan. Things like binge drinking gained a whole other appeal when you'd watched good men get ripped apart by an IED. When you had to watch friends die. He couldn't forget, either, sitting in that damn hospital, staring at Ava's lifeless body, praying somehow she'd wake up.

His date stood quiet a moment. "When'd you get out?"

The soft tone of her voice told him she understood, and he breathed a sigh of relief. This was the main reason he'd opted to go with Military Match. So he wouldn't have to explain to yet another woman why a small dive bar was ten times more comfortable than a crowded nightclub. Or why loud music was akin to sandpaper to his nerves.

"Retired two years ago." He darted a sidelong glance at her. "Why Military Match? Did you serve?"

As she looked over at him, her chin lifted and pride filled her eyes. "No. My father and my brother did. Navy."

"Hooyah." He straightened off the wall and turned fully to face her. "Inquiring minds want to know. Who were you told to meet?"

"Tall, dark, and handsome and..." A slow, cheeky grin spread across her face as she tugged on the corner of his bow tie. "Wearing a blue tie."

"In that case, looks like I'm your man." He gave her a two-fingered salute, then stuck out his hand. "I'm—"

She pressed a finger to his lips, halting the word before he could tell her his name, and shook her head.

"No names yet. Part of the fun of this ball is the anonymity the masks give us, right? I could be anybody. So, pretend I'm your dream girl and dance with me." She didn't give him time to approve or deny the request, but grabbed his hand, tugging him behind her. At the edge of the crowd in front of the stage, she turned to him. "This is a salsa. Do you know how?"

His grandmother had spent hours teaching him and Ava to dance. He knew the salsa...along with the mambo, the waltz, *and* the foxtrot. Not something he'd normally brag about, but the knowledge came in handy every once in a while. Like now.

He listened for a moment, then stepped into the beat, added a few flourishes, including a turn, then winked and held out his hand. "The question is, do you?"

"Impressive." Her grin widening, she took his hand, stepping into the dance with him.

The quick tempo meant he had to concentrate on his steps, on her movements, so that the crowd around him, the music, ceased to exist. There were only those flirty blue eyes and the sway of her hips. He had to hand it to her. She wasn't a beginner by any stretch of the imagination. Her movements weren't stiff, like she followed some remembered set of steps, but fluid, her hips swaying to the natural rhythm of the music like she'd done it her whole life.

The sway of those hips filled his head with more fantasies. What expression would cross those features when her orgasm took hold of her? He had the sudden, overwhelming desire to watch the heat flare in her eyes as her body rose to his...

The song ended far too soon, the tempo slowing to the steady pulse of a heartbeat. The couples around them all shifted, tugging each other closer. Marcus and his mysterious companion stopped moving. She stared up at him, eyes soft, chest heaving with her breathlessness. The need to feel her body against his hit him hard. It had been too damn long since he'd last indulged in the pleasures of the flesh, in the feminine form.

Unable to resist, he lifted a brow. When in Rome... "Shall we?"

When she smiled and nodded, he tugged her close, settling one hand against her lower back. They swayed to the soft strains of the music in silence, movements stiff and awkward, but those blue eyes never left his. Despite the crowd and the overwhelming buzz in his head, the knot that had formed in his gut when he arrived finally loosened.

He released her hand, wrapped both arms around her instead, and pulled her closer. Her small, curvy body swayed against him, her soft belly brushing his with every subtle movement. So close he could feel the hammering of her heart against his chest.

He ducked down, leaning his cheek against the top of her head so she'd hear him over the music. "If you won't tell me your name, at least give me something. What's a nice girl like you doing in a place like this?"

She leaned back enough to peer at him. "I wanted a nice guy. This place has an excellent reputation for the kind of people they accept."

Also why he'd used the service. Not that he'd tell her that. No, he wanted to hear that addicting laugh again. So he tossed her a smile. "How do you know I'm one of the nice guys?"

"Because you served. I've found enough playboys to be able to recognize the good guys when I see them. And most guys who served are the good ones." She averted her gaze to the right. "Just do me a favor, huh? Don't tell me I remind you of your sister. At least not yet. Give me a running start first."

Despite the voice in his head telling him not to say the words, he couldn't resist leaning his mouth beside her ear. "Trust me, angel. What I'm thinking right now has very little to do with my sister."

The tremor that moved through her set his libido thrumming. Marcus stifled a groan. Five minutes with her and already she had his cock swelling against his fly.

It didn't help that when she met his gaze again, those blue eyes filled with an intoxicating combination of heat and challenge. "What *are* you thinking?"

He really shouldn't toy with her, but this was the most fun he'd had in...hell, he couldn't remember. "Oh, I definitely can't tell you that. I'm supposed to be playing the gentleman tonight, remember?"

She let out a quiet laugh. "Well, at least you're honest."

Triumph surged in his chest. It would probably get him into trouble at some point, but he had a feeling he'd make an ass out of himself in order to hear that laugh again. It ought to scare the hell out of him. He'd spent his life determined to keep people at a distance. You couldn't get hurt if you didn't expect anybody to actually stick around. Something about her, though, relaxed his nerves.

He shook his head and chuckled. "Suddenly I'm not sorry I put on this damn monkey suit."

"Me either." She averted her gaze to her right again, but the corners of her mouth twitched. "You look pretty hot in that tux."

He ducked his head, leaning his mouth beside her ear again. It was pushing his luck to say this, but hell, he was going for broke. Just to hear her laugh again would be reward enough. "You're inspiring some very naughty thoughts yourself in that dress."

"Oh, now you're just laying it on thick." Her eyes glinted with playful impishness as she arched a brow. "You didn't actually think it would get you anywhere, did you?"

He let out a dramatic sigh. "A guy can hope."

She laughed again, light and airy, and damned if he could stop from smiling along with her. They spent the rest of the song in silence, somewhere between oddly comfortable and a fine sweet tension that arced between them. It was subtle. More in the shift of her body. She leaned into him and rested her forehead against his chin. He was hard as steel, but if she noticed she didn't say anything or even push away.

"Tell me your name, angel." He wanted to roll it around on his tongue and taste the flavor of it. She intrigued the hell out of him, and he wanted more. A feeling he hadn't had in...shit. Practically forever. Most of the women he dated were temporary, women who didn't want to be tied down any more than he did.

Tonight, though, he'd give himself permission to go with it. Today was the anniversary of Ava's suicide. Finding a weekend hookup had long since lost its appeal, but tonight he needed the company.

Instead of the quiet murmur he'd expected, his companion stopped moving. She stood so still the back of his neck prickled, heat moving over the surface of his skin. Her awareness of him sparked in the air like a living, breathing entity.

He pulled back and winked at her in a vain attempt to set her at ease. "I have to know whose name I'm going to be calling out later."

If she slapped him for that, he'd deserve it, but he *hoped* she'd laugh and then finally relax. When she didn't, when she leaned back instead, her eyes studying his face as if searching for the clues to life, his gut knotted.

He shrugged. "Sorry. Bad joke. You were supposed to call me out for being cocky, tell me how full of myself I am..."

Nothing.

He let out an uncomfortable laugh and stroked her back.

"Angel, if you don't say something I'm just going to keep babbling. Do me a favor and save me from myself, huh?"

Finally, she drew her shoulders back. "Mandy."

The name rolled around in his brain. Lodged there. Another small brunette inserted herself into his thoughts. With similar blue eyes, big and wide in her face, and the softest mouth this side of the Mississippi. He studied his companion's face. The similarities were there, but surely she couldn't be *that* Mandy.

His heart now hammering from the vicinity of his throat, he drew a deep breath and forced a calm that came from experience. He was a SEAL, damn it. One little brunette would not throw him off his game.

He smiled and prayed she didn't notice the way his hands shook. "Mandy's a very pretty name. Got a last name to go with that?"

Again, she stared. Her throat bobbed. Her mask trembled as she reached up and pulled it off her head, revealing her full face.

His heart stuttered to a stop. Son of a *bitch*. So that's why she'd looked familiar—he'd been seeing her in his dreams.

Of all the women in Seattle, they'd fixed him up with the one woman he wanted more than he wanted to breathe . . . and the only woman he couldn't touch with a ten-foot pole: his buddy's kid sister.

CHAPTER TWO

Mandy Lawson fisted her hands at her sides, her body trembling like she stood on the fault line of an earthquake, as she waited for Marcus to say something. Anything. When she'd approached the ballroom ten minutes ago, the sight of him had stopped her in her tracks. He'd seemed familiar. The dark, almost black hair, cropped short. The day's worth of scruff covering his jaw. The width and strength of his chest and shoulders, narrowing down to lean hips and a tight, firm ass even his tailored slacks couldn't hide.

If that fine specimen of male ass wasn't enough to confirm her suspicions, the color of his eyes had blown his cover. Marcus Denali's eyes were as blue as a cloudless sky, yet contained large splotches of golden brown. She'd never seen anything like them before or since.

Marcus pulled off his mask and cocked his head to the side, his brow furrowing. He scanned her face as if seeing her for the first time. Or perhaps like she'd grown another head right in front of him.

Finally, he released her and folded his arms. "Why do I get the feeling you knew it was me?"

The accusation in his tone sank deep, setting her knees knocking together and her stomach churning. Damn it. She wasn't afraid of anything. Not even spiders. Marcus Denali? The guy made her nerves quake.

Mandy squashed it all and squared her shoulders. "Your eyes gave you away."

Marcus scanned her face again and took a step back. "Why didn't you tell me it was you?"

Mandy scratched a nonexistent itch on the side of her head. He had her on this one, but what the hell could she tell him? Not once in all the time she'd known him—and their group of mutual friends got together every chance they could—had Marcus ever looked at her with anything more than impassive regard. What harm would it do to play out the fantasy for a few hours?

She sighed. She had lied to him, though. A lie by omission, maybe, but still a lie. "I wanted one dance before you realized who I was and that look crossed your face."

Marcus's mouth formed a thin line. "What look?"

She nodded in his direction, her heart sinking into her toes. "That one. Like I'm that annoying little kid you tolerate because you have to. When I first realized it was you, I thought maybe Lauren and Steph had set me up. I figured one dance wouldn't hurt before I let you off the hook."

She and Lauren had known each other since junior high.

Steph she'd met five years ago, ironically when Steph hired her to plan her wedding. Unfortunately, Steph had gotten stood up at the altar, and Mandy had made a friend that night. They'd been the Three Musketeers since. It would be just like one of them to give the woman at Military Match a little hint as to who to fix her up with.

"One dance? I'm pretty sure that was two, and unless I'm mistaken, you originally suggested we not tell each other who we were at all. Besides..." Marcus lifted a dark brow, those intense eyes pinning her to spot. "Why would they set you up?"

Heat flooded her cheeks. Mandy diverted her gaze to the floor, staring at anything but him. She had no desire to know what would cross his face when she said the words. "I should think that's pretty obvious by now."

Four months ago, Lauren and Mandy's brother Trent had gotten engaged. Ironically, the two had gotten fixed up through Military Match. They'd celebrated their engagement by throwing a party, friends and family only. One thing had led to another that night, as things often did where alcohol was concerned, and Steph dared her to make a move on Marcus. She'd taken Steph's dare and planted one on him, in front of everybody. Surely a guy like Marcus had enough experience to realize that meant she was into him?

Marcus gave a slow shake of his head, muttering something under his breath she didn't catch. Several seconds ticked by before he finally turned his head and met her gaze again with that infuriating impassive facade. "You're going to have to fill me in, angel, because I'm afraid I'm not following you."

He stared, expectation in his gaze, but her mind had gotten stuck on the nickname. *Angel.* He'd called her that before he knew who she was. Hearing it now had hope rising from the dead, fluttering in her chest like a hummingbird's wings.

She shouldn't ask, but damn it, she had to know. "Angel?"

His eyes searched hers for the span of a heartbeat. Then his gaze flicked over her, to her feet and back up. "I've never seen you in a dress. You're usually in jeans. You look pretty incredible."

For a moment, Mandy could only stare. Holy shit. He'd actually given her a compliment. Giddy awareness shivered down her spine, settling in the expensive silk panties she'd bought for this date. Nobody ever complimented her appearance. She was short, wide bottomed, and small breasted. Not exactly the kind of woman who turned heads. Never mind her frizzy hair.

It didn't help her sexiness factor any, either, that she'd been a tomboy growing up. Her father had been an engineman in the navy, servicing and repairing the ships' big engines. The only way to get some one-on-one time with him when he was home from deployments was to let him teach her. Turned out, she'd enjoyed it. It meant she could guzzle a beer with the best of them and she could do her own repairs on her car. One of the guys, wasn't that what most of them usually called her?

She longed for one man who didn't. Who saw beneath the exterior. Who looked at her the way Gabe looked at Steph— with adoration and desire in his eyes.

The way Marcus had looked at her before she'd taken off her mask.

"Say that again." The words came out this side of breathless, like she was back in high school, face-to-face with Dylan

Pembroke, the guy she'd had a huge crush on all of junior and senior year.

One corner of Marcus's mouth hitched upward. He narrowed his gaze, his eyes dancing at her. "Answer the question. *What* ought to be obvious?"

Her stomach fluttered, along with her knees. She'd been waiting for this moment since Trent and Lauren's engagement. The fallout of that kiss. *You can do this.*

She squared her shoulders and stuck out her chin. No way would she back down from this. "I kissed you, Marcus. I would think the *what* should be pretty obvious."

He folded his arms. "So call me slow and explain it to me.".

She shrugged. "Steph dared me."

Marcus chuckled. "A dare? That's very high school, angel. Why would she do that?"

Mandy's shoulders slumped, dejection sinking over her and pulling at her limbs. Of course he'd laugh. Because she was the tomboy, the woman men liked to hang out with but nobody wanted to *date*. At least, not seriously. Should she have expected anything less from Marcus? Like most of the men she'd dated, he was delicious and one hundred and twenty percent out of her league.

She heaved a sigh and waved a tired hand in his direction. "I wanted to convince Steph to see Gabe, and she needed a little shove, so I made her a bet. Steph's competitive. It was just a joke between friends. I'm sorry if I offended you or crossed a boundary. I'm also sorry I didn't immediately tell you who I was. I had a feeling you'd do exactly what you're doing now. I'm sorry I'm not who you hoped for. Consider me saving you from having to spend the evening with someone who reminds you of your sister."

Heart in her shoes, she didn't bother to wait for his reaction, but turned and strode away from him, heading for the ballroom entrance.

Apparently, she could count tonight's date as another failure. Signing up with Military Match had been her idea. Jennifer Dillon, an old friend from high school, had hired her to plan her wedding and had recommended the service. So far Mandy had had ten dates. Ten. Five of whom she'd gone out with more than once. Who still called to invite her out for a beer...because they now considered her a friend. A freaking friend! That was her, just another one of the guys.

When she reached the elevator at the end of the hallway, Mandy jabbed the down button and folded her arms to wait. She wanted a good stiff drink, something strong, which would warm her belly and leave her delirious by morning.

"Hey!"

Mandy darted a glance down the hallway. Marcus jogged in her direction. Disappointment sank in her stomach. Great. That's what she needed, him to want to continue her humiliation. She punched the button several more times in rapid succession, hoping, somehow, it would speed up the elevator.

When he came to a stop beside her, he leaned sideways, bumping her shoulder. "I offended you. I'm sorry. I'm kind of out of my element tonight. Of all the women I expected to end up with, I sure as hell didn't expect it to be you."

"Yeah, I got that part. Don't worry about it. It doesn't matter." The elevator dinged open. Mandy took the opportunity to get away from him and stepped on, punching the button for the ground floor.

Before the door could close, Marcus stepped in beside her. As the elevator lurched into movement, he tucked his hands in his pockets and looked over at her. "It matters to me."

Heat rose up her neck and into her cheeks. "You're not going to let this go, are you?"

"Nope." He had the nerve to smile at her, all pleasant and sexy as hell. His eyes crinkled at the corners, and her knees melted.

Dragging her courage up from the pit of her stomach, she forced herself to face him. When you hit bottom, there's nowhere to go but up. So she cocked a brow at him. "You want the truth or the sugarcoated version?"

He smirked. "The truth might be nice."

She drew a deep breath and let the words fly. "I kissed you that night because I wanted to. Steph's dare was an excuse. I've been dying to seduce you right out of those worn jeans you're always wearing since the first time I met you. When I realized it was you back there, I could also tell you didn't recognize me, and I wanted to take advantage of that. Truth is, you were flirting with me right up until I took my mask off."

For a long moment, Marcus stared. When regret took shape in his eyes, instinct told her what his response would be.

He reached up, rubbing the back of his neck. "Listen, angel…"

Mandy held up a hand. "Please don't say it. If you have any respect for me at all, you'll let me get the hell out of here without mortifying myself any more than I already have. I had to try, because if you don't ask the answer is always no. Well, now I know."

The elevator glided to a stop, the doors dinging open, and Mandy stepped out into the hotel's lobby. She set her sights on the exit, some twenty feet or so beyond her, and strode toward it without looking back to see if Marcus had followed. Once she hit the street, she turned right and kept on marching. Lauren's bakery sat only a couple blocks from here. At seven o'clock on a Friday night, it would no doubt still be open. She needed her longtime best friend's quiet sensibility and some of that luscious, smooth chocolate she made.

Mandy had gotten only to the end of the block before the soft thud of shoes hitting the pavement sounded behind her. A glance over her shoulder confirmed that Marcus had followed. She lengthened her stride, but just her luck, the light changed, forcing her to stop on the corner to wait. Seconds later, Marcus jogged up beside her.

He nudged with her an elbow. "Would you stop running from me and give me a chance to say something?"

She shook her head. Sighed. "What's there left to say? How you feel is written all over your face, and you know, I'd rather you not say it, if you don't mind. I'd like to save what's left of my self-esteem, thanks."

"Well, I'm going to say it anyway." He tucked his hands in his pockets and turned to stare at the street beyond. "Do you have any idea how old I am?"

She arched a brow and darted a glance at him. "If that's your idea of an explanation, you're going to have to try a bit harder than that."

He turned his head to look at her, one corner of his mouth hitching. "You're a feisty little thing, aren't you?" He arched a brow, those delicious eyes glinting with challenge. "Just answer the question, angel."

Mandy rolled her eyes and waved a dismissive hand at him. "There you go with the confusing sweet nothings. Not helping, Marcus."

Hell. She was behaving like a spoiled brat, but this entire conversation rubbed an already raw nerve.

Marcus remained silent for the span of several pounding heartbeats, then took a step closer, his muscled shoulder brushing her arm. He leaned down, his breath warm on her ear. "Would you like to know *why* I call you that?"

Her heart rate took off for outer space. Who the hell could think when he did that? His scent curled around her, something subtle and woodsy and entirely male, and everything below the waist became hot and molten. She was pretty sure her expensive panties had just vaporized.

She shrugged. If she did anything else she'd be melting at his feet. She sure as hell would *not* look into those hypnotic eyes. "Whatever floats your boat."

This time, his nose nudged her earlobe. His warm breath caressed her neck, setting her heart to hammering like a hummingbird's wings behind her breastbone. Mandy held her breath, afraid to move for fear of breaking whatever spell held them bound. If this was a dream, she had no desire to wake up.

"I'm only going to say this once, angel, so listen carefully, all right? You walk into a room, and I'm blinded by you. In that dress you're a walking wet dream." He chuckled, a quiet rumbling that sent shivers down her spine. "Hell, in a pair of grease-stained jeans, you make me hard enough to hammer nails."

Holy...Did he really just admit he was attracted to her? Heart now hammering from the vicinity of her tonsils, she jerked her gaze to his. Only to bring her face inches from his. Close enough electricity arced between them like the snap of static. His pupils dilated and his nostrils flared, but he didn't so much as twitch a muscle.

After a moment, he straightened, one dark brow lifting. "Now, answer my question. *Do* you know how old I am?"

Mandy swallowed past the thick paste in her throat and waved a hand between them. "I don't know. I figured you were about Trent's age, thirty-eight or so."

He let out a sardonic laugh and turned his head, looking off down the street for a moment. "Forty, sweetheart. I turned forty two months ago. That makes me two years older than Trent and twelve years older than you."

She wrapped her arms around herself and shook her head. "I'm afraid you're trying to convince the wrong person with that argument. My brother Will's wife, Skylar, is five years older than he is, and Trent married my best friend. Lauren's ten years younger than him, in case you didn't realize. So the age difference doesn't bother me, but whatever, point taken."

Both her brothers had married outside their pay grades, as the saying went, and the age difference mattered squat to either of them. A fact she completely agreed with. Marcus had a maturity about him that made him sexy as hell.

Marcus let out an uncomfortable laugh and rubbed the back of his neck. "You're going to make me work for this, aren't you?

All right, angel, I'll spell it out for you. I'm settled and old-fashioned. My idea of a good time is the nightly news and my dog in my lap. I sowed my wild oats a long time ago."

He turned his gaze to the street again. While he appeared relaxed, the stiff set of his shoulders and the tick in his jaw gave away his discomfort.

"Your brother also works for me. I have a strict code of ethics I follow to the letter, the top of which is that I don't date co-workers. Or my buddy's kid sister. The guys who work for me aren't just employees. They're friends. So I stay away from you because—"

Finally having heard enough, she cut him off by holding up a hand. "Stop. Please. I get it. You're not interested." She rolled her eyes, because if she didn't at least pretend flippancy, she'd cry. And damn it, she wasn't a crier. "I'm sorry I put you in an awkward position, and I'm sorry you got stuck with me tonight."

The light changed for the third time, the green walk sign blinking from across the street. This time, Mandy jogged out into the crosswalk, only slowing once she was halfway across.

One more date that ended the same way all the others had. *I'm sorry, but...* Up until now, Marcus had been a lovely fantasy, something delicious to keep her warm at the end of the night, when she went to bed alone. His quiet apology, the regret in his eyes a few minutes ago, had shattered the illusion she'd held tight to. The possibility.

Marcus had reminded her how pathetic she was. She was a phony. She planned weddings for a living, helped couples make their fantasies come true, but *her* Prince Charming had either gotten lost or had forgotten her address. Well, screw Prince Charming. She didn't need him anyway.

CHAPTER THREE

Marcus stood on the sidewalk, staring into the small bakery, unable to make himself go inside. He'd officially become a stalker. Following Mandy here was pathetic.

Inside Lauren's Chocolates and Pastries, fluorescent lights made the shop glow against the dark night, lending the place a warmth that made him want to go inside. The small store sat on the corner in a strip mall a few blocks from Pike Place Market. Trent stood behind the counter with Lauren, his hands in his pockets. Across the counter, Mandy leaned a hip against the glass surface. The three looked cozy, like they were having a chat over coffee.

Marcus swallowed a groan. He should turn around and go home. If he went in there, Trent would know something was up between him and Mandy, and he had no desire to explain it. He only wanted to clear the air with her, but he couldn't deny that the thoughts playing through his mind had very little to do with talking. No, they had everything to do with discovering how fast he could get her naked.

She could've bowled him over with a feather when she'd pulled her mask off earlier. His chest had filled with a mixture of elation and dread. Since the afternoon she'd walked into the motorcycle repair shop he co-owned with Gabe, Mandy had become a craving he couldn't shake. More than a year had passed since he'd come to realize she was Trent's kid sister, but time hadn't curbed his hunger for her in the least. Rather, every time the gang got together and he had to see her, be near her, it only increased.

How many nights had he lain in bed, cock in his hand, easing the ache she'd created simply by laughing? He wanted things with her that weren't his to want. That kiss four months ago had been perfunctory, little more than a peck, but oh how he ached to learn more. Like the flavor of her breath. Or the erotic slide of her tongue against his. Thanks to their dance tonight, he now knew the light in her eyes when she looked at him and the way her small, supple body felt moving against his.

Now he had to go inside that building and face her brother.

He couldn't leave, either. Not without at least attempting to explain his reaction. The dejection in her eyes when she'd walked away from him five minutes ago had guilt eating at his stomach. He wasn't good with words. Never had been. And all his fumbling had done was hurt her. So he might not be able to act on his feelings for her, but he wouldn't be able to sleep tonight if he didn't at least clear the air. At the very least, she deserved to know she'd assumed all the wrong things.

With a resigned sigh, Marcus pushed into the shop and halted inside the doorway. All three heads turned in his direction and every inch of his body tensed as he waited for reactions. Mandy's eyes widened. Trent had the nerve to grin at him. Great. Mandy had clearly told them who her date tonight was.

Marcus forced himself to focus on Mandy. "It had to be this place, huh?"

Mandy shrugged. "My best friend owns this shop. I got all dressed up for a date that didn't pan out. Figured *somebody* might want to have a drink with me." She straightened away from the counter and folded her arms. Her eyes narrowed. "Stalking me now, Marcus?"

The mistrust and hurt in her voice made his shoulders slump. If that didn't confirm his suspicions, he didn't know what would. He *had* hurt her, and she *was* pissed at him. Rightly so.

He darted a glance at Trent, who stood watching the two of them with a curiosity that made his gut clench. There was no easy way about this. Any move he made now would clue Trent in that something had happened between them. If Mandy hadn't told him herself.

Marcus dragged a hand over the back of his neck. Hell. He might as well get it over with, because he wasn't backing out now.

He released the door and strode farther into the shop with a casualness he didn't feel. "I wouldn't have to stalk you if you'd stop storming off. I wasn't finished."

Mandy closed her mouth, a very becoming pink suffusing

her cheeks. Trent let out an amused snort, but at a glare from Mandy, swiped a hand across his mouth and turned his head, taking a sudden interest in the back wall.

Marcus crossed the space between them and took her hand. "You're coming with me."

When he pivoted and strode back toward the entrance, she didn't offer a protest, which was good, because he wouldn't accept one.

"Just remember, Denali," Trent called to him as he reached the entrance again, his voice full of amusement. "I know where you live."

Unable to face his friend, Marcus kept going. He was breaking a rule, goddammit.

"Talking, Lawson. That's all we're doing." He gave an exasperated shake of his head and pulled open the door, sending the chime dinging again. "And possibly coffee, because God knows, I need some sort of kick to deal with her."

Trent chuckled. "Trust me, man. Whiskey's better."

Mandy jerked her gaze to Trent, eyes narrowed. "Hey."

Trent laughed and held up his hands. Marcus ignored them both and pulled Mandy outside, moving down the street at a full stride. As soon as they hit the sidewalk, the muscles in his shoulders tightened and his gut knotted. He was now alone with her. With only his conscience to keep him on the straight and narrow.

God help them both.

Halfway down the street, she tugged on his hand. "Marcus, I'm wearing four-inch heels. Would you slow down?"

He halted mid-stride, drew a deep breath in an attempt

to calm his jangling nerves, and forced himself to face her. A full momentum going, Mandy stumbled into him, ending up in his arms when his hands shot out to steady her. For a moment neither one moved. She settled her warm palms on his pecs and stared at him, eyes wide and this side of stunned. He didn't know if he even remembered to breathe. This was, what, the third time tonight she'd ended up plastered against him? He had no desire to let go. Exactly why he should.

"I'm sorry." He narrowed his gaze on her, as if somehow she were to blame for the fact that he couldn't resist her. "You make me crazy."

Hell, he couldn't think straight around her period. She made his cock ache. God, he'd kill for a single weekend with her, simply to satiate his lust for her. That was why he always avoided her whenever the gang got together. He flat out didn't trust himself.

Who was he kidding? He didn't trust himself now, either, because the trouble was, were she anybody else, he wouldn't hesitate to scratch that itch.

What he expected from her he couldn't be certain, but amusement glinted in her eyes. "Ditto."

"I'm trying to find a more secluded spot." He glanced over her head at the street behind her. The sidewalk was full of people all moving toward their destinations. Two shops down, a giggly threesome of girls entered a jewelry shop. A small crowd waited on a corner for the light to change. A block away, the Starbucks sidewalk café was full. Where in all of this would he ever find a private spot to chat?

"For what?"

The suspicion in her tone made him look at her. She stared at him, brow furrowed, surprise in her gaze.

He frowned. "Don't look at me like that. *If* I were to make love to you, it most certainly would not be in public."

Shit. He shouldn't have said that. Now the blasted images were parading through his skull like an erotic slide show. Her soft body pressed against his. Skin on skin. He could almost hear the cry she'd let out when she came . . .

As if she could read his thoughts, heat flared in her eyes. "Actually, sex in public can be pretty hot."

Those words from her perfect little bow-shaped mouth had his imagination running on overtime. All too easily he could envision her, skirt hiked above her waist, back pressed against the brick building, riled up by the possibility of getting caught. His cock tightened, thickening against his zipper.

He dragged a hand through his hair. Jesus. She really would be the death of him. He'd die of sexual frustration, from lack of oxygen to the brain.

Spotting an alley between two buildings, he tightened his hold on her hand and pulled her into it. Once out of sight of most passersby, he pressed her back against the building. "This will have to do, because I don't trust myself with you anywhere we could actually be alone."

The corners of her mouth twitched, but her chest rose and fell at a rapid pace. "Again, you wouldn't hear me complaining."

He braced his hands on the brick beside her head, because if he put them on her, it was all over. He'd silence her sassy little mouth by possessing it, and then God help them both, because he didn't think he could stop there. "I hadn't intended to follow you, but I hurt you again with what I said, and that doesn't sit well with me. Since clearly I'm not making my point well enough, I'm going to try this one more time."

Mandy blinked, eyes heavy-lidded and burning through him. "I'm listening."

Despite his best intentions, the warm breaths puffing against his mouth had him caving like a starving man in a sandwich shop. He leaned down, hovering over the soft temptation of her. "It isn't a matter of whether or not I'm attracted to you."

Mandy sagged back against the wall and rolled her eyes. "You're beating around the bush, Marcus. Trying to tell me something but not actually saying the words. Just say what you mean."

God, what was it about the sound of his name on her lips? He wanted to hear her moan it, preferably in the throes of an orgasm *he'd* given her.

Talking. They were only supposed to be talking. But nothing he'd said so far had come out the way he'd intended. He was fumbling, damn it. So he latched on to the first idea to flit through his mind: stop talking and *show* her.

He leaned into her and rocked his throbbing erection into the softness of her belly. "That clear enough for you?"

Mandy let out a quiet gasp, her fingers curling into his chest, and Marcus gritted his teeth. She felt so fucking good, soft in all the right places. He ached to rub his engorged cock over every inch of her warm skin. Christ. If he ever had the pleasure of her sweet body beneath him, his first time with her would no doubt be hard and fast and over in minutes. He'd probably blow his top the moment he slid into her.

"Make no mistake about it, angel." Unable to resist touching her, he tucked a curl behind her ear. She had naturally curly hair, thick and coarse, but surprisingly soft, like the rest of her. God how he wanted to burrow his fingers into it. "It's all I can do to not think about you. Ending up with you tonight wasn't a disappointment, but more of a *holy shit* moment."

One dark brow rose, but amusement glinted in her eyes. "Holy shit? That's not exactly flattering."

He let out a miserable laugh and dragged a hand through his hair. Could he screw this up any more? "You really don't get it."

Mandy's cheeks flushed. "You're my tenth date. I've made quite a lot of friends through Military Match. Every single man was truly a nice guy, but there was no chemistry with any of them. I've started to wonder if it's me."

Idiots. They were all idiots.

His fingers curled against the brick with the irritation sliding along his spine. Since the night she'd kissed him, every single guy he heard about her dating had gotten the same reaction. The idea of seeing her with one of them filled him with the burning desire to deck the jerk, toss her over his shoulder, and carry her back to his cave.

He leaned down, touching his nose to hers, so there would be no mistaking his meaning this time. "Any man who can't see what a phenomenal woman you are doesn't deserve you."

He forced himself to straighten before he did something he'd really regret. Like possess her mouth. Simply to make her forget everyone but him. To satiate the hunger burning a path through his blood. "The thing is, angel, I'm still way too old for you."

"Again, not a problem for me." Mandy mumbled the words under her breath, but loud enough he caught them. When he narrowed his gaze on her, she rolled her eyes. "Shutting up."

The corners of his mouth twitched. God she had fire, and damned if it wasn't the sexiest thing about her.

He skimmed his fingertips along the curve of her collarbone and swallowed a groan. Another touch he shouldn't have allowed but couldn't resist. She had the most incredible skin, so warm and smooth. Like butter beneath his fingers. What he wouldn't give to wrap himself up in it.

He pulled his hand back. *Focus, damn it.*

He drew a breath and tried again. "You go clubbing on a regular basis. You grab life by its ears. I'd bore the hell out of you."

Mandy let out a harsh laugh. "I sincerely doubt that."

She really hadn't a clue. They were night and day and he wasn't anything she needed.

"Once upon a time, I *was* you. Out drinking and partying until all hours of the night. Waking up with a hangover. These days, my life is a whole lot simpler. I enjoy the small things. My dog greeting me at the door at the end of a long day. Dinner on Sundays with Gram. And yes, occasionally, the company of a woman. I like sex slow and I choose my companions carefully."

Hell, he was rationalizing at this point. The truth was, any other time, he'd want a woman exactly like her, someone who could hold her own. She saw her tomboy tendencies as something negative, but that was sexy to him. But he also needed someone who'd be okay with his life choices.

"Relationships aren't my thing, angel. I don't believe in love, and I have no desire to get married."

The whole notion left a bad taste in his mouth. His parents had gotten married right out of high school because his mother had gotten pregnant. His father had been an angry, bitter man, resenting his and Ava's presences. Not long after his seventh birthday his father ran off with a prostitute, of all things. His mother drank to escape, and then one day, when he was around ten, she dropped him and Ava off with their grandmother and never looked back.

The idea of getting married turned his stomach. It meant someday having kids, and he had no desire to risk scarring another human being. Hell, he already knew he wouldn't be any good at it. Ava's bipolar disorder had meant he'd had to take care of her, often as if she were a wayward teenager, and in the end, he'd failed her. Six months into his last deployment, Ava took her own life. Her death had only proven what he already knew.

"I'm not somebody to be relied on." He stroked his thumb across Mandy's chin, allowed himself a moment to get lost in the softness of her skin. "If I keep my relationships light, then nobody gets hurt."

Mandy's gaze searched his face, as if she were trying to figure him out somehow. "And yet men have. SEALs are teams. You rely on each other."

He grunted his acknowledgment. She had him there. Being a SEAL was the one thing he'd done well. Hell, he'd thrived as a SEAL. The challenge and teamwork. But even there, he'd lost friends. Too damn many of them. And like Ava's, every death hung on his soul.

Confusion filled Mandy's eyes. "So why use a dating service, then? What did you hope to get out of it?"

"Because I'm human. I get lonely, too, and a one-night stand just doesn't do it for me anymore." He released a heavy breath. "What I need is someone I can see for a while. Someone my grandmother will like."

"Wait..." Mandy cocked her head sideways. "You sought out a dating service to make your grandmother happy?"

He rubbed the back of his neck. Yeah, okay, so it sounded as pathetic as he'd assumed.

He stared out into the street beyond, watching the passing cars. "My grandmother's the reason I am who I am, that I ended up where I did and not in a jail cell. I was a rotten teenager. Rebellious. Cocky. I'd gotten in with the wrong crowd and Gram yanked me out by my ear. She saved my damn life. Last year, she came down with pneumonia. Since then, she's been laying on the guilt trip, telling me how much she wants great-grandbabies and wishes I'd settle down. The way I see it, the only thing that will make her happy is if she thinks I'm attached."

"You want something temporary."

He made a sound of agreement from the back of his throat. "I need someone I can bring to Sunday dinners, who'll pretend to be my girlfriend but won't expect anything from me.

I need Gram to know I'm fine, and she won't stop worrying unless she sees me with someone."

Mandy's intense gaze burned into him, but he couldn't force himself to look at her. He had no desire to know what played in her eyes. Instead, he idly watched the car lights flicker over the buildings they passed.

"And if I offered to be that someone?"

He jerked his gaze to hers. Had he heard her right? "Why would you do that?"

"Because I think it's sweet that you want to. Not very many men would go through so much trouble for their grandmothers." She shrugged and laid a tentative hand against his chest. "It means you have a heart in here. That's sexy in my book."

He glanced down to where her small hand lay against his chest. Three layers of clothing separated them: his dress shirt, the T-shirt underneath, and a thick suit jacket. He ached to strip it all off just to feel those soft hands on his skin. For the simple pleasure of feeling her body against his again.

Mandy drew a shuddering breath. She slid her hands around his rib cage and up his back and leaned into him. Damned if he could stop his arms from coming around her in turn, or keep himself from leaning down and brushing his lips across hers. Holy Christ, she had the softest mouth.

Mandy pulled back first. Eyes still heavy-lidded and burning through him, she stepped out of his embrace and walked backward toward the street. "I'll play the part of your loving significant other, have Sunday dinners with your grandmother, whatever it is you need. But I want one thing."

He shouldn't ask the question seated on the tip of his tongue, but something in his gut demanded the answer. "What's that?"

"Nights with you. Think about it." She winked at him, then pivoted and strode out onto the sidewalk, disappearing around the corner of the building a few pounding heartbeats later.

Marcus could only stand and stare. Just like that, with a few simple words, she'd brought all his fantasies of her screaming to the forefront of his thoughts. Temptation stared him in the face, and the effort it took not to follow her, not to drag her back into the alley, press her against this damn building and hike that skirt up around her waist, had his body a mass of tension. His shoulders ached. His hands fisted at his sides. His blood roared in his ears. Son of a bitch. She had to go and lay that offer on the table. Right then, he couldn't think of one damn good reason why he shouldn't take her up on it.

CHAPTER FOUR

I'm telling you, sweetie, you need to seduce that man."

Mandy didn't answer Steph, but instead downed the shot of tequila. She took a moment to enjoy the unique flavor and the warmth spreading through her belly before peering across the table at Steph. "Yeah, 'cause that's worked out well for me so far."

After leaving Marcus in the alley an hour ago, she'd headed straight back to Lauren's bakery. One phone call later, she and the girls now sat in one of the clubs downtown. Any other night, this place would have been exactly her style. Music with a strong beat vibrated the walls, daring you to get up and shake what your mama gave you. The DJ worked the crowd like a boss. The whole place had an energy that on any other night would have had her among the crowd packed on the dance floor.

Mandy picked up a wedge of lime, sucked the juice from the fruit, and set the rind on her napkin. Discovering Marcus was attracted to her too had been a heady lure she hadn't been able to resist. An hour and two shots of tequila later, however, doubt twisted through her stomach. "I should not have propositioned him like that."

Steph frowned. "Why the hell not? You've wanted him for years."

"Because he isn't anything I need at this point in my life." Mandy braced her elbows on the table and ducked her head into her hands. "God, me and my big mouth. I took one look at the desire in his eyes and the words just...popped out."

That he'd held her crushed against his big, solid body hadn't helped, either. Marcus might be forty, but he was firm all over. Never mind the impressive erection that had pushed into her belly. His mouth brushed hers, and her imagination ran away with itself. In seconds flat, her panties disintegrated.

Steph sipped at her glass of Moscato. "Exactly why you should stand by your offer. Take the time with him and enjoy the hell out of it. Consider it a fantasy lived. Trust me. You'll regret *not* doing it a whole lot more than you'll ever regret doing it."

"Chances are, he'll turn me down, and I'll just end up feeling like an even bigger fool." Mandy picked up another shot and downed it, the liquid adding to the warmth spreading through her limbs. "All I want tonight is to be delirious enough to forget I even made that offer."

Seated beside Steph, Lauren curled her hand around her glass of soda. Four months pregnant, she'd volunteered to be their designated driver. "He hasn't said no yet, sweetie."

Mandy chuckled as she set the third empty shot glass beside the others. "He hasn't said *anything* yet. I made the offer, then tucked my tail between my legs and hightailed it out of there."

"Put on something low-cut and do your thing. Clearly, he wants you, so"—Steph winked at her over the rim of her wineglass—"give him a little incentive."

"That's very underhanded." Mandy let out a laugh that sounded half crazed even to her own ears and sipped at her beer. She really would need a ride home after this. A lovely little buzz floated through her head and tense muscles began to unravel.

"No, it's not. You're just giving him a little nudge. You know..." Steph set her wineglass on the table and leaned her elbows against the edge, blue eyes gleaming with playful impishness. "Gabe wants to throw a barbecue next Saturday. He plans to invite the guys from the shop, which means Marcus will be there. Perfect chance to woo him."

Lauren looked over at Steph, eyes taking on a knowing gleam. "If you're inviting the whole gang, does that mean we're celebrating something?"

Steph looked between the two of them and sighed, slumping in her seat. "It's been such a long week. I haven't had a chance to touch base with you guys. I had court this week, a nasty custody battle. By the time I get home at night, I'm beat."

"Uh-huh. You sure it isn't Gabe making you tired?" Mandy tossed Steph a grin and reached across the table, nudging Steph's hand. "Spit it out already."

Steph grinned, plunked her chin in her left hand, and turned her head. She drummed her fingers nonchalantly against her cheek. "Notice anything *different*?"

"'Bout time. I've been staring at that since we got here." Mandy snatched Steph's hand, brushing her thumb over the gorgeous solitaire. A cushion-cut diamond set in rose-colored gold. Simple yet stunning. She peeked up at Steph, offering her friend a more heartfelt smile. "Gabe has good taste."

Lauren nudged Steph with an elbow. "Congrats, you."

Steph, normally all no-nonsense lawyer and about as fearless as they came, flushed to the roots of her blond hair. "He proposed last Saturday."

Mandy's heart swelled. Blinking back tears, she tossed Steph a smile. "I'm so happy for you."

She wanted to be jealous. Both of her best friends had found their other halves and here she was, forever the bridesmaid, but she couldn't drum up the emotion for the life of her. After being stood up at the altar, Steph deserved to finally be happy, and Gabe gave that to her in spades.

Lauren glanced at Steph, brows raised. "How's his daughter taking the news?"

Steph glanced at her ring for a moment. "Surprisingly well. Gabe wants to include Char in everything and said she helped pick out the ring. Apparently, he'd chosen something else and she vetoed it. Said she liked this one better. He wants a long engagement, and"—Steph turned to Mandy, shooting her an apologetic frown—"no offense, sweetie, but we're going to do the wedding ourselves. Char wants to help, and we'd like to include her."

Mandy squeezed her fingers. "No offense taken. If you need any help or any contacts, let me know."

Steph clasped her hands together and flashed a sheepish grin. "I do have one request."

Mandy nodded. "Anything for you, babe."

Steph straightened in her seat and pulled her shoulders back. "I'd like you to design my dress."

Mandy blinked, her heart thumping dully against her rib cage. "Me? Sweetie, I've got a ton of contacts with shops who do fabulous work. It's been a while since I've done a wedding dress."

And even then only a handful of times and always with the watchful eye of the shop owner.

Steph's gaze traveled over her. "You designed that dress you're wearing now, didn't you?"

Mandy glanced down at herself. Once upon a time, she'd entertained the idea of becoming a famous fashion designer. Had gone to school and gotten her degree. Had even done a couple summer internships in a small bridal shop. Wedding planning had come almost by accident. A friend had asked for help. Word had spread. Turned out she did it well. She'd never regretted following her heart.

Steph was right, though. She still dabbled in fashion design. She had drawings all over her apartment and had sewn more than a few of the items she wore on a regular basis.

She finally looked up at Steph and gave a helpless shake of her head. "What if I screw it up?"

"You won't. I trust you. Please? Say you'll do it?" Steph shot her a smile and winked. "I want a Mandy Lawson original."

Mandy nodded and sniffled. "I'm honored, sweetie. Truly honored."

"Thank you. We have a while to work on this. Gabe wants to give Char time to get used to the idea." Steph picked up her drink and winked again. "Now, about you and Marcus...take no prisoners, sweetie. I've seen the way he looks at you when he thinks nobody's watching. He'll cave. I promise."

Mandy furrowed her brow. "You're right. If I back out now, I'll look like a coward. And I'm a lot of things—impulsive, tomboyish, too upbeat for my own good—but I'm *not* a coward."

Besides. She could flirt with the best of them. When she wanted to scratch a primal itch, she had no trouble picking up a date in a club. Could she do that with Marcus, though?

She could. And she would. Steph was right. If she didn't, she'd regret not trying.

Bolstered, Mandy lifted her beer in salute. "Looks like I'm seducing a SEAL."

Steph laughed softly. "Go get him, honey."

* * *

Marcus looked up from the grill, peering across the expanse of the rectangular yard to where the guys from the shop and their significant others gathered for Gabe and Steph's engagement party. Mandy sat beside Lauren at one of the two tables set up in the yard.

Seven days had passed since their date from Military

Match, and he hadn't been able to concentrate all damn week. Hell, since she arrived an hour ago, his brain function had been shot to hell. It was why he was hiding out behind the grill—because he couldn't stop remembering her offer. Or kicking himself in the ass for not immediately taking her up on it.

She had to go and look gorgeous tonight, too. The pink top she wore amounted to a thin scrap of silk held up by spaghetti straps. It didn't help that her puckered nipples pushed against the material. The knowledge had his imagination going nuts. Was she even wearing a bra? Were her breasts sensitive? Would she let out that maddening little whimper when he stroked his thumbs across those straining tips?

"Thanks for helping with the cooking, Marcus."

At the sound of the soft voice, Marcus jerked his gaze from the vision across the way and turned a nervous smile on Lauren. A plate of potato salad in one hand and a beer in the other, she stood smiling at him, a knowing, slightly amused glint in her eyes. His heart hammered his rib cage. Crap. Had she caught him staring?

"Not a problem. I enjoy it." He nodded in the direction of the tables, where Gabe sat with Steph on his lap, resting his chin on her shoulder. "Gives those lovebirds a chance to relax."

"Well, I appreciate it. So do Gabe and Steph. Though I did notice you seem to be keeping to yourself." Lauren's keen gaze worked his face. "Is it the crowd or the music?"

Heat flooded Marcus's face. Lauren seemed to have taken the lot of them under her wing. She came to the shop regularly with goodies from the bakery, always making sure they took the time to stop and eat.

He shook his head and tossed her a rueful smile. "Apparently, I'm not holding it together as well as I'd hoped. It's a little of both. I enjoy the hell out of these get-togethers, but..." He shrugged.

She nodded, as if she somehow knew, understood. "Crowds give Trent a headache. I'll go turn the music down. We'll probably call it an early night. With Charlotte being at her aunt's tonight, I'm sure Gabe would rather have Steph all to himself anyway."

He chuckled and nodded. "I'll stay and help clean up."

"I appreciate it." She jerked her head toward the house. "Pull those ribs off, and then go grab a beer and relax. That's an order."

"Yes, ma'am." He saluted her with the tongs, watching for a moment as she approached the table across the yard.

Lauren took a seat, setting the beer in front of Trent and the potato salad in front of Gabe and Steph. She nudged Mandy and leaned over, whispering something in her ear. Mandy turned that blue gaze on him and smiled, then picked up her plate and rose from the table, sauntering in his direction.

His gut knotted. Crap. Apparently, he *had* been caught staring. When Mandy actually stopped beside him, his heart launched itself into his throat.

"Hello, Marcus."

Just the sound of her voice, soft and velvety with a touch of humor and familiarity, had his cock standing up and saluting her.

"How you doing, Mandy?" Marcus kept his gaze on his task. If he looked at her, he was done for. His heart hammered his freakin' rib cage, for crying out loud. Like he was seventeen. The soft heat of her body beside him launched a thousand fantasies, most of which revolved around her, naked beneath him.

"Just Mandy? I'm not your angel tonight?" She *tsk*ed and bumped his shoulder, her voice taking on a teasing lilt. "Have to say I'm disappointed."

Okay, she got him with that. He glanced at her... only to wish he hadn't. She stood pushing her bottom lip out, but she looked so damn cute doing it he couldn't help laughing. He shook his head and looked back to the grill. "Put that thing away. No fair pulling that lip on me."

She leaned toward him, so close now her scent swirled around him. Even over the smoke and meat, the aroma of vanilla wafted around him, daring him to bend his head to her neck. "But it's working, isn't it?"

Marcus forced himself to focus on turning over the last batch of ribs. What he needed to do was give her the cold shoulder and let her walk away. This was Mandy, damn it, and her brother sat barely twenty feet away.

He couldn't help himself, though, and made the mistake of glancing at her again. Her eyes glinted with mischief, and for a moment, he was caught in that sparkling gaze. He'd never get used to her looking at him that way, with such unrestrained hunger. Up until Lauren and Trent had gotten together, he'd rarely seen Mandy. Just the few times she'd come into the shop for parts for her bike. His attraction to her back then had been easily squelched.

Now, with them all getting together so often, he saw her on a more regular basis. Had gotten to know *her*. She was the oddest mixture of shyness and strength. Soft and feminine with a huge heart, but tough around the edges. Mandy was different, in a way his whole body sat up and took notice of. She'd become a craving he couldn't shake.

Now here she was, and despite the voice of reason telling him not to say it, the words were leaving his mouth anyway. "If that's your attempt at unsettling me, you're going to have to try harder than that."

She had the nerve to grin and wink at him. "Oh, challenge accepted, Mr. Denali. Challenge accepted."

Drawn completely into the playful banter now, he couldn't help himself here, either. He turned his head and narrowed his gaze on her. "It's Marcus, if you please."

She arched a brow, eyes glimmering with a potent mixture of heat and amusement. "You get to call me angel, but I only get to call you by your given name? How's that fair?"

He chuckled. God, he loved that fire.

"Fine, angel. Call me whatever you like." Unable to help himself, he leaned his mouth beside her ear. "But play nice."

She drew a shuddering breath. The shiver that moved through her made his cock twitch, begging him to drag her off into a dark corner somewhere. Never one to be deterred, however, she locked her hot blue gaze on his, fire flashing in the depths. "How 'bout 'stud'?"

He tipped his head back and laughed, because if he did anything else, he'd be pulling her into the house. "You are something else, you know that? Can I actually get you anything? Or did you come over here just to taunt me?"

Mandy laughed, her body relaxing beside him. "Actually, I was sent over here to save you from yourself. Lauren says you're isolating." She playfully batted her lashes at him. "Am I helping?"

He *was* isolating. Manning the grill was an excuse. He damn well didn't trust himself around Mandy. She was candy, and he was a starving kid.

"No." He narrowed his gaze on her. "Because *you're* not playing nice."

She grinned again, completely pleased with herself, and waggled her brows. "So I am getting to you."

He shook his head. "You always have."

The little minx had the nerve to lean toward him, her voice lowering to a conspiratorial murmur. "Do tell."

The husky tone of her voice, low and sensual, slid along his nerve endings and landed right in his jeans. He pivoted toward her. Remembering the others seated nearby, he stopped just shy of dragging her against him. He clenched his jaw, the muscles in his shoulders tensing to the point of aching. "Angel?"

Mandy froze in front of him, blinking up at him with wide, stunned eyes. "Yeah?"

He kept his voice low enough the others wouldn't be able to hear. "There's a reason I'm hiding behind this grill, and you're it."

She drew a shuddering breath that damn near undid all his good intentions. "So you *have* considered my offer."

He lifted a hand, stroking it along her forearm. Some part of his brain blared a warning, but he *needed* to touch her. Just once. "I've thought of nothing else *but* you this week. Keep pushing and find out what happens when I lose control of myself."

He'd meant his comment as a tease, hoped somehow she'd ease up on him, but Mandy, little hellcat that she was, squared her shoulders. She pulled herself to her full height and closed that last step between them, standing so close her breasts brushed his chest. "You don't scare me. I've thought about you, too. I'm pretty sure your name left my lips more than once this week."

His mind filled with the exact images she'd nonchalantly hinted at. Her lying naked on her bed, thighs spread, her fingers slipping into her velvet heat. The huff of her breath as she grew closer to orgasm. The sound of his name leaving her lips on a quiet moan as she tipped over the edge and began to tremble...

Marcus swallowed a groan and forced himself to turn back to the grill, his jeans suddenly two sizes too small. "Not helping, angel."

Mandy took the tongs from his hand, pulled a half rack from the low-heat side of the grill and set them on her plate, then handed back the tongs. Apparently not done tormenting him, she pulled a bit of meat off the end of one rib and popped it in her mouth, her cheeks hollowing as she sucked on the tips of her fingers.

"Mmm. Your ribs are delicious. This is my second helping. You know, I could never be a vegetarian. Like my meat too much." The little firebrand winked at him, her gaze falling to his crotch. "Looking good in those jeans, by the way."

Before he could gather his wits enough to form a coherent response, she turned to saunter away. She left him standing there watching her phenomenal ass swing and trying to remember why it was he couldn't have her.

* * *

Leaning against the wall, Marcus drummed his fingers against his thighs as he stared at the bathroom door across from him, willing the damn thing to open. After pulling the last batch of ribs from the grill two hours ago, he'd done exactly as he'd promised Lauren and joined the fray. Mandy hadn't stopped teasing him since she walked away from him. Every time she came near him, her fingers would trail his lower back or graze his arm. More than once those luscious breasts brushed against him as she squeezed past him on her way to something. And the heated looks across the table? Christ.

Her teasing had been funny at first. Cute. From any other woman, those sorts of obvious ploys did nothing for him. From the one woman he craved but couldn't—shouldn't— touch? No cold shower could possibly douse the flame she'd lit in his gut. She had him wound so freaking tight he was half afraid he'd do something he shouldn't.

Which was why he was here, stalking the bathroom instead of getting that extra beer he'd come inside for. Mandy had gone in there a few minutes ago. He intended to nip her over-the-top behavior in the bud. Before he went fucking insane.

The bathroom door opened with a whoosh of air disturbed and a quiet squeak. Mandy stopped short in the doorway, eyes widening with surprise. "Marcus."

Determination swelled behind his breastbone. He straightened off the wall and closed the distance between them in two long strides. One hand braced on her chest, he pushed her back inside the bathroom, closed the door, then rounded on her. She hit the door behind her and froze. Her chest heaved, those big blue eyes wide in her face. She looked stunned.

Good.

He reached out to engage the lock mechanism on the doorknob, then set his hands on either side of her head and leaned down. Every muscle in his body tensed with the effort it took not to seize her sassy little mouth.

"If you wanted my attention, angel, you've got it. I've been hard all night no thanks to you." He had a hard-on nothing would deflate. Except maybe her hands. Or her mouth. Or...

Mandy had the nerve to grin at him. She lifted onto her toes, bringing her mouth so close her warm breaths teased his lips. "So what're you going to do about it?"

The amusement glittering in her eyes scraped his last sane nerve.

"What I want..." He slid his hands to her ass, lifted her off her feet, and pressed her back against the door. His aching cock settled against her heat, and he leaned into her, let her feel the result of her teasing. "Is to fuck you against this door."

His intent had been to warn her, to scare her enough she'd do what he clearly couldn't and walk away.

Except her breathing hitched and her eyes slid to half-mast. Mandy locked her legs around his hips, her heels digging into his ass as she pulled him closer. Her voice lowered to a whisper. "I'm yours, Marcus."

Like a fraying rope straining to hold the weight of something beyond its capabilities, his last ounce of willpower snapped. He claimed her perfect mouth and rocked his aching erection into the heat emanating from between her sweet thighs. Her fingers slid up the back of his neck and into his hair, and she moaned softly, her mouth opening beneath his. Like a man dying of thirst, he drank her in. He wanted to devour her, to possess her.

Her hot tongue reached back. The quiet little moan emanating from the back of her throat vibrated between them. Her aggressiveness only fueled his need for her.

Desperate to touch her, he held her securely with one arm and slid the other up her stomach and beneath the hem of that silky top. When his fingers closed around a warm, satiny globe, Marcus groaned. "Christ. You really aren't wearing a bra."

His mind took that one small detail and ran with it. Was she wearing panties? Or had she gone commando, too? The thought of her ass bare beneath those form-hugging jeans made his balls ache. All he'd have to do was strip her of those jeans and he could be inside her in less than a minute.

He nibbled his way across her jaw and down her neck, any part of her he could reach. In the recesses of his brain, a red alert blared, but Mandy let out another moan, this one filled with need and desperation. It lit him up like a match to a dry field. The yearning to hear her make that sound again increased tenfold, and he flicked his thumb across the tightened tip of her breast. The gasp she let out had his chest expanding and triumph storming through his system.

"This is what you do to me, angel. I want my mouth and my cock on every inch of you. Christ you feel so fucking good." He pushed his hips into her, for the sweet pressure of her against him, and skimmed his lips across her bare shoulder. Her vanilla scent filled his nostrils with every breath he dragged in.

Mandy panted in his ear, her supple lips skimming his jaw, as her hand skimmed down his belly. One rough tug and she had his fly open. A breath later, she slid her hand inside. When her fingers closed around his throbbing erection, every muscle in his body tensed. He locked his knees to keep himself upright.

"Shit." He groaned again. "Careful, angel. You have me really wound up."

If she'd even heard him, she gave no indication. Instead her warm, supple fingers tightened around him. While some part of his brain told him to stop this before it went too far, her hand glided over his engorged flesh, and everything narrowed down to that intimate connection. He rocked into her hand, every stroke hurtling him toward the luscious abyss so fast he lost his breath.

A final glide of her fingers over the now super-sensitive head had his orgasm slamming into him. He pressed his face hard into her neck and held his breath, shaking uncontrollably as he emptied himself into the warmth of her hand.

Marcus dropped his forehead onto her shoulder as he attempted to catch his breath. "I give, angel. You win."

CHAPTER FIVE

The words left Marcus's mouth with little thought, but as he stood there, his come in Mandy's fist and her fingers caressing the head of his now softening cock, the truth settled over him. He wanted everything she represented. Freedom from the past. The chance to step into something beyond the meaningless sex he'd had for so damn long it had lost its appeal.

He also wanted the chance simply to spend time with her. Maybe he'd satiate his lust for her and get it the hell out of his system. Whatever the reason, he didn't have it in him to resist her anymore.

Mandy went still and silent for a long, unnerving moment. It wasn't fair to tease her by being deliberately vague, but he couldn't force his true answer from his mouth. Guilt was already knotting his gut. He'd come tonight to celebrate Gabe and Steph's engagement, not to seduce Mandy. His closest friends—including Trent—all sat within shouting distance.

Mandy leaned her head against his cheek, her breath erratic and warm in his ear. "I win what?"

"Me." He finally forced himself to lift his head.

Mandy stared, eyes wide and searching his, like she couldn't believe he was actually agreeing, and an exposed feeling rose over him again. How the hell she did it, he hadn't a fucking clue, but she had him on his knees. One tiny woman made him feel like he was naked and exposed, as if everything tender was exposed to the elements. Only one other woman had ever come close. "You're accepting my offer."

"Yes. I'd be lying if I said I haven't spent the last week kicking myself in the ass for letting you leave that alley."

She cocked a brow, as if she didn't quite believe him. "May I ask what made you decide? A week ago you were adamant this wasn't something you could do."

He touched his nose to hers. "Maybe I just can't resist you. Ever think of that?" He lifted a hand, tucking a lock of hair behind her ear. "I do have to ask, though. Why would you settle for a guy like me?"

Her brows rose. "A guy like you?"

He was going to have to spell it out for her. He'd done it a thousand times, made sure the woman he was with knew in no uncertain terms he wasn't relationship material. So why did the thought of telling Mandy—and having to watch her reaction—suddenly make his stomach knot?

Either way, he needed to be honest with her. Needed her to know, to understand, where he stood in this.

He sighed. "I'm not anything you want or need, angel. I decided the day my mother dropped me off at my grandmother's and never came back that relationships weren't worth it. I've lived my life every day since determined never to need anyone."

He'd had one serious relationship in his life, and he'd fucked that up, too. Emma had ended things before his last deployment. Was it really five years ago now? He regretted everything about their time together. She'd wanted a ring, but the thought of being tied down gave him the cold sweats. Too well he remembered his parents' marriage. The constant fighting. His mother's drinking. And him and Ava sinking into the background, unnoticed. The whole institution didn't seem worth it to him. To put each other through that kind of torture or torture their kids? Nope. He wanted to keep his relationships light.

Now here was Mandy, throwing a wrench into his carefully ordered world.

"Frankly, angel, you're pushing boundaries I set a long time ago. I mean, look where we are." He glanced around, taking in the toilet and the sink, the mirror and the blue shower curtain. The moment he'd arrived at collapsed on top of him, guilt weighing on his shoulders like a sixty-pound pack. "I cannot believe we're in a freaking bathroom."

"You're too hard on yourself, Marcus." Mandy's expression softened, her fingers skimming his cheek. "People get caught up in a moment all the time. Maybe things moved faster than we intended them to, but it happens."

"Not to me it doesn't." He turned his head and met her gaze, stared and waited for the fallout of his pathetic confession.

Of all things, amusement glinted in her eyes. "So, what, sex is to be done in the dark?"

For a moment he could only stare. She was laughing at him, but she was so damned beautiful doing it, the corners of his mouth twitched with his effort to hold back a reciprocating grin.

He rolled his eyes. "Yeah, okay, go ahead and laugh and get it out of your system. I was raised by a woman who comes from a whole different world, a whole different value system. I'm old-fashioned. So sue me."

Mandy dropped her gaze to his chest and settled her clean hand there, her palm warm, thumb stroking back and forth. "I'm sorry. The confession just surprised me. I thought maybe your reaction the other night was because of me. I grew up roughhousing with Trent and Will. When Dad was home, I spent as much time as I could with him, which means I can keep up with men on a lot of levels. Most of the men I've met seem to find that intimidating. Or at least...not sexy."

Irritation punched him in the gut, and his fingers curled against her ass. What he wanted to do was deck any and all assholes who'd made her feel that way. The last thing she needed, though, was him acting like a jealous damn boyfriend. So he pulled from years in the service and drew a deep breath, tamping it all down.

Instead, he immersed himself in her and stroked his thumb over her chin again, brushing across her lower lip. "Clearly you've been dating idiots, because if you ask me, angel, that's sexy as hell. But the truth is, you *are* different for me."

She rolled her eyes. "Yeah, like I haven't heard *that* before."

He stroked his thumb across her cheek this time. Hell, he couldn't help himself. He'd spent more than a year trying not to feel anything for her. The simple luxury of getting to touch her at all was a bit like opening the floodgates. He wanted to touch *all* of her.

"No, I mean it. You've always been off-limits, and not just because of my friendship with Trent. I happen to like you. You have guts. You aren't afraid to go after what you want. That night you kissed me? You surprised the hell out of me. I had a hard-on all damn night."

He'd never forget that night as long as he lived. Her soft mouth had barely grazed his, but the determination and hunger in her eyes had made for a sleepless night. He'd ended up with his cock in his hand, satisfying his overwhelming desire for her in fantasies. Her soft body beneath him. Her legs locked around his hips. Her hot breath in his ear.

He followed the curve of her jaw with his thumb for a moment, imagined following the path with his mouth. "Now, answer my question. Why would you settle for a guy like me?"

She smiled, soft and alluring, shy yet bold and cheeky. A smile he was coming to think of as uniquely her own. "I don't see it as settling. I see it as taking a chance. I told you, when I signed up with Military Match, I hoped to find a nice guy to date for a while, someone who wouldn't be turned off by my tomboy tendencies." She dropped her gaze, her voice lowering to a heartfelt murmur. "Someone who made me feel . . . beautiful. Feminine."

What she wasn't saying set his teeth grinding against each

other. How the hell any sane man could see her as anything less than fucking phenomenal was beyond him.

"Idiots. The lot of 'em." He'd meant the comment as a reassurance, but the words left his mouth on little more than an irritated grunt, laced with the jealousy currently seeping through his blood. He wanted to prove to her that not all men were like the asshats she'd found. To be the one to make her realize how beautiful and sexy and feminine she already was.

Her gaze flicked to his, those eyes reaching and searching. She smiled, one side of her mouth lifting higher than the other. Her hand smoothed across his chest.

"I'll be honest with you. Am I hoping to find something more, like what Trent and Lauren have?" She shrugged. "Yeah. Someday I am. Frankly—"

He shook his head, tension knotting his shoulders. "That won't ever be me, angel."

She pursed her lips, shooting him a reprimanding frown. "Would you let me finish?"

The corners of his mouth twitched with his effort to hold back his grin. There was that fire again. God he so loved that fire.

He forced a serious face and made a zipping motion across his mouth.

"As I was saying...I also want *you*. I haven't made that a secret. I consider this a way to live out a fantasy." The corners of her mouth twitched as she looked down, her fingers teasing his skin as she traced the shop logo on the front of his T-shirt. "All I ask in return is that when it ends, you don't tell me I remind you of your sister. And please, for the love of my sanity, don't play the *let's be friends* card."

He ducked his head, leaning his mouth to her ear. Because he wanted her to know, to hear in his voice, that he meant what he was about to say. "I told you on that date, the thoughts that run through my head every damn time I see you are definitely not of the sisterly sort."

A shiver moved through her, and she let out a breathless gasp, her fingers curling against his chest. Marcus groaned softly and nipped at the pad of flesh where her neck met her shoulder. That one small reaction made him so damn hard it hurt.

He forced himself to pull back enough to see her face. This next part was important. "I would like to put some boundaries on this, though."

She sighed and rolled her eyes, those wicked fingers of hers toying with the hairs on the back of his neck and driving him to distraction. "Of course you'd have rules. All right. Lay 'em on me."

"This is only for a month. I'm not going to need more than that to convince my grandmother. When the month is up, this ends. All of it."

He had every intention of diving headfirst into his time with her. At this point, if he was going to hell anyway, he might as well enjoy the ride. He'd fulfill his own fantasies and get her out of his system once and for all.

"We want the same things, something out of the norm, but I've lost too many people in my life. The guys at the shop are important to me. They're family, and you're a part of that." He leaned down, touched his nose to hers. "I don't want to lose that."

"You and your principles." She rolled her eyes, but one corner of her mouth quirked upward.

He shrugged. "Part of the package, angel."

"Fine, but I have a few demands of my own."

He nodded. It was only fair. "All right."

She furrowed her brow, her expression suddenly serious, as if she were preparing for a fight from him. "When I said I want nights, I meant *all* night. No sneaking out while I'm asleep. If you can't stay long enough to have coffee with me in the morning, don't bother."

How many assholes had actually done that to her? "Any man who sneaks out while you're sleeping is a goddamn coward who needs to grow a pair."

She laughed quietly, amusement illuminating those gorgeous blue eyes. "Is that so?"

"Yes." He blew out a breath, releasing his irritation along with it, and stroked his fingers down her cheek. "For the record, that's not my style. I have never and will never treat a woman like she's little more than a warm body, and any man who does doesn't deserve the time you've given him."

"I'm glad we agree." She gave him a tender smile, braced her hand against his chest, and rose onto her toes again. This time, she caught his bottom lip in her teeth. "Now that that's settled, how 'bout we meet next Friday after work? Because I believe you owe me an orgasm, and I'm afraid to tell you, Mr. Denali, I'll be adding interest."

A door opened and closed somewhere in the house. Logic told him he needed to end this now, before they got caught, but damned if he could resist.

He leaned down, flicking his tongue against her earlobe. "Trust me, angel. I have every intention of leaving you breathless."

The little minx rocked her hips into his again, grinding against an already growing hard-on. "I'll be holding you to that, you know."

He groaned and captured her mouth. Allowed himself a moment to enjoy the flick of her tongue, her hot breath mingling with his, then forced himself to pull back. If he didn't, he'd do something stupid. Like forget her brother sat just outside and fuck her against this door.

His breaths coming harsh and fast, he leaned his forehead against hers. Forced his mind to focus. Jesus. He had a feeling he'd come away from this month exhausted. "I'm afraid Friday's no good for me. I have a veterans support group on Friday nights."

The teasing light left her eyes, to be replaced with a soft concern as she laid a hand against his chest. "Do you still have trouble?"

He didn't have to ask to understand she was talking about PTSD. Every guy he'd served with came home with some form of it, and he'd been no exception.

He shook his head, his forehead rocking against hers. "Not too much. Fireworks make me jumpy. I can't stand crowds or loud music. The usual stuff. But for the most part, it's eased. No, I've taken over the running of the group. Some of the guys are fresh off a deployment and they're deep in it."

Like the young soldier who'd just joined their group. Jason was barely twenty-five and had come home from his second tour in Afghanistan a month ago. He was having a hell of a time of it but refusing help. Given his reluctance to talk, Marcus worried about him. Too many held it in, fearing they'd be seen as weak.

"I need to be there."

"Then it'll have to be Saturday." Mandy gave a curt nod, then jerked her head at the door behind her. "We should get back out there before someone comes looking for the bathroom."

"And catches us together." He made a sound of acknowledgment from the back of his throat. A cold chill traveled the length of his spine, his body already missing the heat of hers.

Awkward awareness of each other prickled in the air as he did up his pants and Mandy washed her hands. When she was done, she returned to him, though, and pressed a soft kiss to his lips.

"See you Saturday. My place okay?" When he nodded his agreement, she pecked his lips again and disappeared out the door. Seconds later, she poked her head back in. One dark brow lifted, as if she were about to put him on the spot, but the corners of her mouth twitched, betraying her. "And you just better have your A game on."

He chuckled. Oh, he'd have his A game on. And his B and C as well. He'd have fun seeing how many times he could make her come before she waved the white flag. If he was going to break all his damn rules to spend a month with her, he had every intention of enjoying the hell out of it.

He winked. "Oh, I intend to, angel. I intend to."

CHAPTER SIX

When the doorbell sounded through the apartment the following Saturday night, Mandy's heart skipped a beat. A thousand butterflies took flight in her stomach, a heady mix of nerves and anticipation. God. Marcus was here.

She eyed her reflection again, smoothing a trembling hand down the front of the light-pink blouse she'd put on ten minutes ago. Truth was, nothing about this fling was wise. After all, it was a complete detour from the reason she'd signed up with Military Match in the first place. Because she wanted what Lauren had found with Trent. What Steph had found with Gabe.

But she had to take the chance or live to regret it. She had no intention of letting Marcus become an "if only." At least this way she'd come away with memories she'd look back on with fondness.

The doorbell sounded again, pulling her from her tangled thoughts, and she turned away from her reflection, trotting barefoot down the hallway to the apartment entrance. She stopped a moment to draw a deep, calming breath, then pulled the door open.

As expected, Marcus stood on the other side. Hands tucked in his pockets, he looked delicious in a pair of well-worn jeans and a black T-shirt that molded itself to his upper body. He smiled, heat flaring in his eyes. "Hey."

Feeling too much like a child on Christmas morning, she barely managed to stand still and fisted her hands at her sides. "You actually came."

One dark brow rose. "You doubted?"

She could only shrug, heat creeping into her cheeks. Okay maybe she had. She'd had a week to ponder this moment, to drive herself crazy. So many of her dates from Military Match had failed and her ego had taken a beating. She hadn't expected her plan to seduce him to actually work.

He stepped over the threshold and pulled her close, then leaned down, hovering over her mouth. Every breath teased her skin. His heady scent curled around her senses. "Then you should know I've spent the last week with a hard-on. Every time I think about you, about this, the damn thing pops up. Besides, I believe I owe you an orgasm."

A hot little shiver meandered its way down her spine, landing straight in her panties. Her clit throbbed in delicious anticipation. "What did you have in mind?"

His mouth brushed hers, so lightly she lifted onto her toes, leaning into him in an effort to get more of him. What she wanted was for him to claim her mouth. To leave her delirious and breathless, the way he had in the bathroom last week.

He seemed to have his own ideas, though, because he hovered beyond reach, sipping here, tasting there. Always light, like he had all the time in the world to do only that.

"You said you thought of this as like living a fantasy. I say that's a good idea, playing out fantasies." His gaze flicked to hers as one finger stroked the shell of her ear. "Tell me your favorite."

She nipped at his bottom lip. "Clearly you haven't been listening. You."

The left corner of his mouth hitched. "How, exactly, angel?"

A quiet, ragged breath escaped her. He had her eating out of the palm of his hand, and the cocky gleam in his eyes said he knew it, too. Damn, he was potent like this. "Any way I can get you."

He rocked his hips against hers again, pushing a very solid erection into the softness of her belly. "Tell me *how*."

Her fingers curled against his chest. "Your hands. Your mouth. Your cock. Any of it. All of it."

"Details, please. You said you thought about me last Friday night." He leaned his mouth beside her ear, his voice a hot whisper against the sensitive lobe. "When you slid those fingers into that hot little pussy, what were you thinking about?"

"God, I love it when you talk to me that way. Your hands. You have fantastic hands. Strong and masculine, and you have these wonderful, rough calluses. When you slid your thumbs over my nipples?" She closed her eyes for a moment, immersing herself in the memory that filled her thoughts. "God, it felt incredible. So last night I imagined you sliding these warm, rough fingers over my clit."

A thoughtful little *hmm* of pleasure vibrated out of him. When she opened her eyes, he was staring at her, eyes heavy-lidded and hotter than hell itself. "You thought about me last night?"

"I couldn't help myself. *You* got relief at the barbeque. I've been simmering on a low boil ever since."

He drew a sharp inhale, his nostrils flaring. "Damn. You're killing me here, angel. Now to decide...what to do with you...what to do with you..." His voice came low, his gaze following the tender stroke of his thumb across her lower lip. After a moment, he lifted his head and peered around him. "Do you have a full-length mirror?"

She frowned. Where was he going with this? "Yes. On the back of my bedroom door. Why?"

"I have an idea. Come on. Let's go see about repayment." He brushed his mouth over hers, little more than a lingering tease, then took her hand and strode toward the back of her apartment. Halfway there, he passed her dining room and stopped. He stood staring for a moment, then hooked a chair in his free hand and continued down the hall.

"What's that for?" she asked.

He shot a wink over his shoulder. "You'll see."

Everything from the neck down trembled as she followed him. How many times over the years had she fantasized about exactly this? That he'd lead her to her bedroom and strip her naked. In those fantasies, he always teased her with those strong hands and that sexy mouth.

God. The simple thought of being pressed against his bare skin had everything below the belt hot and molten, yet every step made her knees shake. For all the wrong reasons. Nervous, antsy reasons that gave her the vague sensation of being a virgin. Like she had no idea what the hell she was doing. It was one thing to pick up a lover in a club. There, she could be whoever she wanted to be. Girly and coy. Confident and carefree. Aggressive and dirty.

But Marcus knew *her*. He'd seen her in grease-stained jeans, a baggy T-shirt, and no makeup, and somehow, he was still here.

It would be miracle if she didn't make a dork of herself and scare him off.

Once inside her room, Marcus closed the door, strode about five feet, and set the chair down. Then he moved to stand behind the chair and rested his hands along the back. "Perfect."

She followed his gaze to the mirror, and a hot little shiver rocketed down her spine, landing in her quickly dampening panties. Their reflection gave her an inkling why he'd brought the chair, and her imagination took *that* little tidbit and ran with it.

"Somebody has a kinky side." She grinned and sauntered in his direction, making sure to add some extra swing to her stride.

An action he most definitely caught, for his gaze dropped and his nostrils flared. God, she'd never get tired of that look. Not many sober men looked at her that way. Like she was beautiful.

His gaze flicked to hers again. He shook his head, amusement dancing in his eyes as he met her around the front of the chair. "I'm not normally, but something about you seems to bring it out in me."

When she stopped in front of him, he snaked an arm around her waist and tugged her against him. She settled her hands against his chest, his body warm and deliciously solid beneath her palms. She ought to say something seductive, keep the thread of conversation going, but her brain shorted and all she could think of was "Hi."

"Hi." His intense gaze scanned her face as his fingers stroked torturous circles over her lower back. "I have to admit, now that I've got you here, I suddenly can't think for the life of me. Least, not about anything except stripping us both naked, tossing you onto that bed over there, and sinking into you."

Her core throbbed in eager anticipation, and Mandy smiled. She shouldn't say the words seated on the tip of her tongue. It was teasing. Neither could she resist.

She slid her hands up his back and pressed closer. "I believe I've told you this before. You wouldn't get any arguments from me."

"Don't tempt me, angel. You've had me wound up for days." He growled low in his throat, an entirely male sound filled with frustration and needs denied. His big, warm palms closed over the globes of her ass, and Marcus tugged her hard against him. He bent his head, teeth gently nipping at the muscle where her neck met her shoulder. "I'm not sure I could be gentle with you."

The image filled her mind's eye. This big body pinning her

to the mattress as he surged into her so hard her headboard knocked the wall. A quiet moan escaped her. God, he was so potent like this, almost arrogant, playing the bad boy. Marcus was a SEAL, polite and honorable to his core, which meant this cocky show was all for her, and the knowledge had her clenching in need.

"I won't break, you know." She sagged against him and rocked her hips into his. Damned if she could resist the pull of him. "A little roughness in the bedroom can be fun."

Marcus chuckled, the sound little more than a sexy rumble against her throat, and lifted his head. His eyes filled with a mix of desire and amusement. "Is there anything you *haven't* tried?"

She opened her mouth to respond, but Marcus silenced her by claiming her lips. There were no tender sips this time. Instead, he cradled her head in his palms, tilted it to the side, and plunged in. Nipped with his teeth. Sucked on her bottom lip. He possessed and demanded a response, and she was helpless to do anything but give him one. Mandy fisted her hands around his T-shirt to keep herself upright and gave as good as she got. God, the man could kiss.

When she was a puddle at his feet, he finally released her, and she opened her eyes. He had the nerve to wink at her. "Well. Now I know how to make *you* properly submissive."

While some part of her brain urged her to toss something cocky back at him, all she could do was stand there and try to catch her breath, to get her legs to hold her upright. All sensation had pooled between her thighs. Heat prickled along her skin. Her nipples tightened to the point of aching. One kiss and he had her eating out of the palms of his hands, his to do with as he pleased.

And that damn grin said he knew it, too.

She sighed. "Marcus?"

His gaze dropped, following the torturous stroke of his thumb along her now sensitive bottom lip. "Hmm?"

"Naked." She settled her hands on his lean hips for leverage and lifted onto her tiptoes, catching his bottom lip between her teeth. "Now."

"I'm sorry." The impish glint in his eyes suggested he wasn't sorry in the least as he skimmed his fingertips along the outside curve of each breast. "Am I driving you crazy?"

A wave of heated, shivery goose bumps moved over her skin, from the point of contact outward. A quiet gasp escaped her, and damned if she could stop herself from leaning into his touch.

She dropped her forehead to his chest with a quiet laugh. "Okay, okay, point taken. You win. I give."

"I'm sorry. I can't help teasing." He chuckled again, looped his arms around her, and ducked his head. His voice came as a hot murmur against her ear. "I happen to like the playfulness between us."

So did she. Getting naked with a man for the first time could be damn nerve-racking. That it was Marcus made it even more so. His teasing, though, disarmed her and made her feel comfortable with him.

Not that she'd tell him that. It would only serve to pump his already inflated ego. Instead, she smoothed her hands over his chest, found his nipples, and stroked her thumbs across

the hardened tips. She'd always wondered if they were sensitive. There was something so sexy about a man with sensitive
nipples. When Marcus dragged in a hissing breath, triumph
surged through her system. Oh, she'd have fun with that.

He lifted his head, eyes narrowed in playful retribution.
"You'll pay for that."

"Promises, promises." She pushed her breasts into his chest
and tipped her head back. "Now, please. For the love of my
sanity. I'm yours. Whatever you have planned? Get on with
it. My panties are soaked. I *ache*."

"Minx." He groaned and brushed his mouth over hers, then
released her. After taking a seat in the chair, he waved a finger
at her. "Shirt. Off, please."

She cocked a brow and planted her hands on her hips. "I
suppose women always do what you tell them to?"

The corners of his mouth twitched, but to his credit, he
didn't grin this time. "Yes. Now, if you don't mind, take it
off. I can tell you aren't a wearing a bra, and I'd like to see
those gorgeous breasts I had my hands on last weekend."

The hunger in his eyes made her obey. Gaze locked on
his, she gripped the hem of her shirt in trembling hands and
pulled it off over her head, dropping it to the floor at her feet.
"What now?"

He didn't say a word. Rather, his hot gaze skimmed her
body. She fisted her hands at her sides, forcing herself to stand
there and let him look, but her stomach clenched with nerves.
God, she hated this part, waiting for a man's reaction to seeing her naked for the first time.

"Fucking incredible." The words left his mouth on a murmur as he reached down and adjusted the distinctive bulge in his pants. Seconds ticked out as he stared before his gaze finally returned to hers. "Jeans next, please."

Her breath caught. When he looked at her like that, she actually *felt* beautiful. Not the small, defeated girl inside, who'd been laughed at and tossed aside one time too many for enjoying the things boys did. Sports. Cars.

Mandy nodded and reached for the button on her jeans. His gaze took in every one of her movements as she opened the button and slowly pulled down the zipper.

Remembering all the wiggling she'd had to do to get into these pants, she stopped there and moved to stand between his knees. Without his help, she'd make a complete and utter dork of herself, but if she played her cards right, maybe she could make this something sexy. "I can't take these off without sitting down. I'm going to need help."

He nodded, and she gripped the waistband, pushing her jeans down her legs. Then she laid a hand on his shoulder for leverage and lifted a foot. Marcus skimmed his hand down her thigh and into her pant leg, pushing it down and over the curve of her heel, then held his hand out for the other. When he pulled her second leg free, she kicked her jeans aside and stood, letting him look again.

Like last time, he sat back. His gaze raked down her body, then stopped at the level of her hips. Softness and heat mixed in his eyes as he fingered the edge of her panties. "I like these."

The panties she'd donned this morning were a more feminine version of men's boxers. She wasn't a girly-girl when it came to underwear. She preferred comfort. Every once in a while, though, she wanted something that made her *feel* pretty. This pair was the best of both worlds. The heat in Marcus's eyes made her suddenly glad she'd splurged. "Me too."

The corners of his mouth twitched as he settled his hands on his thighs. "Now take them off."

She swallowed down the nervous lump in her throat, pulled out her confidence, and saluted him. She managed to shimmy out of her panties without falling over and tossed them at his chest. When they landed in his lap, she fisted her hands at her sides again and waited. She was completely bare before him. For the first time. He had a view of every curve, every lump and bump. Now she had to watch his reaction.

Sucking up the last of her courage, she moved to stand between his knees again. "Whatever are you going to do with me now, Mr. Denali?"

A slow grin curled across his face. He grabbed her by the hips and turned her back to him, then pulled her onto his lap. As she settled against the warmth of his chest, he wrapped his arms around her and ducked his head. "Payback."

The husky, almost cocky timbre of his voice sent a shiver raking through her. Her breathing hitched. Her pulse beat a staccato. Mandy swallowed to wet her dry throat and nodded in the direction of the mirror. "So what's that for?"

His nose nudged her earlobe, and his hands skimmed across her abdomen, over her mound, and down the front of her thighs. He gripped her legs, lifting and opening her as he set them on top of his. Then he rested his chin on her shoulder, his low growl rumbling against her back.

"Tonight is all about you, but it doesn't mean I can't have a little fun in the process." His stubbled cheek rasped hers as he nodded. "Look."

She turned her head, peering at their reflections in the mirror, and her earlier nerves flitted away. With her legs straddling his thighs, she was essentially opened to his gaze. It suddenly made sense what he wanted, what *he* got out of this. He wanted a ringside seat to her pleasure. They really did have the same kink. He was a watcher.

She dropped her head back onto his shoulder, limbs limp and heavy as a need moved through her, so keen her clit throbbed. "God."

"I take it you approve?" His lips closed over her earlobe as he skimmed his fingertips over her body. Up over her mound and her belly. Around the sides of her breasts. So lightly every part he touched set fire to her nerve endings and sent a shower of heated, shivery goose bumps along the surface of her skin.

She let out a garbled moan, gripped his right thigh and squeezed, using the solid feel of him to anchor herself.

He chuckled in her ear. "Thought you might."

As his large, warm hands moved along her skin, every muscle in her body tensed, waiting, anticipating his next touch. He took what felt like forever simply stroking her body, exploring her but never making contact with where she ached for his touch the most. He caressed her inner thighs, thumbs grazing her slit so lightly her legs trembled. Walked his fingertips around the outsides of her breasts and around the tops, skimming her areolas but never touching her painfully erect nipples.

She let out a quiet moan and squeezed his thigh again. "Touch me."

He nipped at her earlobe. "I am."

An impatient, frustrated growl escaped her. She took his hand, guided it down her body, and curled his fingers over her mound.

He chuckled. "Desperate, angel?"

God that nickname. To call her angel when they were teasing and flirting was one thing. But here? When she was naked on his lap, spread out for his viewing pleasure? It made her shiver. That name on his lips gave her a sense of possession.

She released his thigh and turned her head, rested her forehead against his cheek. "Marcus, please. You're killing me. I've been wet since you got here."

"That's the whole idea." He caressed a finger up her slit, grazing her clit along the way. At her quiet gasp, he turned his head, his soft slips skimming her earlobe, voice warm in her ear. "Payback, remember?"

Mandy moaned softly. He was getting his payback in spades, and she wasn't above begging at this point. "You win. I get it. I'll never tease you again."

"I've wanted you for a long time, Mandy." Voice sobering, he pressed a finger into her folds and stroked her, making come-hither motions. Pleasure burst along sensitive nerve endings. "I'm enjoying just being able to touch you."

Mandy gasped, her hips bowing into the sweet connection. She'd been right. The calluses on his fingers created the most delicious mix of sensations. Rough yet smooth, combined with the luscious heat of his skin. "God, yes."

"Watch." His husky voice, filled with need, rippled through her, settling in her core, and she obediently opened her eyes, peering at the mirror. In the reflection, Marcus's gaze caught hers, full of a hunger that made her throb, as he plunged one long finger deep inside of her.

The rough warmth of his skin sent pleasure erupting through her. He slid that digit slowly in and out of her, and her mind filled with fantasies. What would it look like if that were his cock? If he fucked her in this chair, in front of the mirror?

His thumb grazed the tip of her swollen clit and the thought flitted away as heat and delight burst along her skin. Every inch of her burned. His erratic breath huffed in her ear as he pumped into her. He had her wound up like a shaken bottle of soda. The pressure built behind her pelvis, the familiar tingle starting at the base of her spine. At any second, the top would pop off and she'd blow, and every inch of her body tensed, waiting for the moment, for the luscious rush of orgasm.

Mandy groaned and closed her eyes, dropped her head back onto his shoulder and gave herself over to his expert fingers. There was definitely something to be said about an older, more experienced man. He hadn't fumbled around trying to find her every erogenous zone, like he had no idea where they even were. Like most of the men she'd been with. No, his sure fingers had zeroed in on them, one by one, stroking her for optimum pleasure.

Until she was bucking in time with his thrusts. She gripped his thigh hard in a vain attempt to root herself, to somehow tell him what she didn't have the frame of mind to say.

One warm palm curled around her right breast. He kneaded the tender flesh, alternating between flicking and pinching and stroking the nipple. All the while his finger pumped faster and faster. Every stroke inside of her glided along a sensitive bit of tissue that sent her reeling toward release. His roughened palm grazed her now throbbing clit again and again.

Every nerve ending came alive, as if he'd lit a match to every exposed, sensitive bit of her.

Another glide along her clitoris and the dam inside of her burst. Her orgasm exploded through her, a shower of hot sparks and a rush of liquids. A wave that washed over her and sucked her under, leaving her shaking and gasping and riding his hand.

He caressed her through every last blinding pulse, until she finally collapsed, breathless and panting, against his chest. Every limb felt like it weighed five hundred pounds. She couldn't catch her breath for the life of her. All the while Marcus continued to strum her body, his touch little more than a tender caress now. The sides of her breasts. Down her belly. The insides of her thighs.

When she finally began to descend from the high and awareness trickled in again, an insane, half-cocked giggle escaped her. "Holy hot damn. I am so keeping you."

His quiet chuckle was warm in her ear as he pulled his fingers from her. "I take it you approve?"

"Oh, I most definitely consider that payment in full." She

turned her head, trying, as best she could in their current position, to see his eyes, and reached back, curling her fingers around the nape of his neck.

He cupped her cheek in his palm and settled his mouth over hers. She plunged her fingers into the short, incredibly silky hair at the back of his head and drank him in. His tongue stroked hers. His teeth nipped, lips warm and surprisingly supple. It had to be the most erotic kiss she'd experienced, slow and deep and so tender she melted into him all over again.

When he finally came up for air, his chest heaved as hard as hers. He nipped at her bottom lip one last time, murmuring against her mouth, "I'm not done with you yet."

CHAPTER SEVEN

As Mandy slid from his lap, Marcus leaned forward, intending to get up. He *wanted* to lay her down on that bed over there, spread her supple thighs, and bury his mouth in her luscious heat. He wanted to taste her, to make her come again and again. Before his desires overcame him and pushed him into caveman mode.

And before the doubts nagging at the back of his mind threatened to unravel him. How wrong it was to want her this much. How right it felt to be this close to her.

He firmly shoved aside the guilt parading through his mind and managed to get to his feet before Mandy rounded on him. She braced a hand against his chest, lifted onto her toes, and nipped at his bottom lip.

"Uh-uh." Her warm hands slid beneath his shirt, pushing it up his chest. "It's your turn. Take this off."

He considered arguing, for the joy of seeing that spunk light in her eyes, but he reached back over his shoulder and did as he was told. He liked this bossy side. It was damn sexy.

He dropped the shirt to the floor. "What next, angel?"

Mandy's gaze raked over him, heat and appreciation in her eyes. Her hands followed, smoothing up his belly and over his chest, before stilling on his pecs. Somberness filled her eyes as she smoothed her thumb over the quarter-sized patch of scarred skin on the corner of his shoulder. A healed-over bullet wound. "When did you get this?"

The tender stroke of her fingers sent a shiver through him. "About four years ago. We were clearing a building when insurgents ambushed us. Fucking sniper got me."

Her brows knit together, worry edging her gaze. "Lucky it only went into the muscle. It could have done a lot more damage."

He made a sound of acknowledgment at the back of his throat. So the doctors had told him.

She smoothed her fingers over the scar again, then leaned forward and pressed a kiss to the wound. Just that small contact, her incredibly soft lips brushing his skin, had a shower of goose bumps popping up along his arms.

Marcus groaned. "There's one on my thigh if you'd like to kiss that one, too."

She gripped the button on his jeans, popping it free. "That can be arranged."

She didn't bother to wait for his approval or denial, either, but slid down the zipper. Then she sank to her knees, taking his pants and shorts with her, effectively freeing him. Eye level with his cock now, she peered up at him. When she actually pressed a kiss to the scar on the center of his right thigh, every muscle in his body tensed to the point of aching.

"Fuck." He dropped his head back as sensation bombarded him: her lips grazing his skin, inches from his throbbing erection, her warm hands on his thighs. He gritted his teeth. "Keep it up, angel, and the fireworks are going to come a lot sooner than you hope."

He expected her to laugh, to toss some cocky comeback at him. The play between them was arousing as hell. She'd made him laugh, taken him out of his head and away from the guilt and regret he hadn't a fucking clue what to do with.

Instead of a tease, however, her soft fingers caressed the scar. "How'd you get this one?"

He opened his eyes. She stared at him, somberness written in her gaze. He traced a thumb along her left eyebrow, his chest growing heavy with the weight of the memories pressing down on him. He'd lost his best friend that day. "I was seventeen and at the wrong place at the wrong time. Got caught in gang war crossfire."

She studied him, eyes reaching and searching, for so long his chest tightened. He half expected her to want the story. Instead, she rose to her feet and pressed her body into his. Her warm, soft skin hit his. Her puckered nipples pushed into his chest, and his control slipped another notch. "What do you *want*, Marcus?"

What he *wanted* was for her to stop looking at him like that, like she could see all those dark places inside. He *wanted* to forget the past. Instead, it lived and breathed inside of him, like a dark entity seeping through his system.

And then there was her. Her subtle vanilla scent curled around his senses. The warmth of her skin and the luscious curves pulled at him, and he let it push aside everything else. She was dangerous in so many ways, and he had no desire to hurt her, but for this month, he wanted to lose himself in her sweetness.

So he slid his hands down the front of her thighs, let his fingers graze her slit and pushed in enough to skim her clit. When her breathing hitched, he leaned his mouth beside her ear.

"What I *want* is to bury my mouth between these thighs. To make you come so hard you clutch my head and moan my name." He flicked his tongue against her earlobe, delighting in the shiver that moved through her. "And believe me, angel, you will."

Her quiet, breathy laugh made his chest swell in triumph.

"You are so full of yourself. You'll just have to wait." She braced a hand against his chest and shoved.

He hit the edge of the chair, teetered, and dropped. "Apparently, you're in charge tonight."

"That's right." Eyes glittering with a potent mixture of mischief and desire, she slid onto his knees and leaned forward, rubbed her breasts against his skin, and whispered into the space between them, "This mirror gave me an idea."

"Oh yeah?" He grabbed her hips and tugged her closer, until her wet heat settled against his aching erection. "What's that?"

She gasped, and a shiver moved through her, but Mandy slid her hands up his chest and rocked her hips, grinding against him. "I thought we'd fuck in this chair."

That word from her wholesome little mouth had his cock twitching. Her suggestion, however, filled his mind, and he jerked his gaze to their reflections. "In front of the mirror."

She flicked her tongue against his bottom lip. "Uh-huh."

The realization sank over him. He returned his gaze to hers and grinned. "Someone else has a kink."

Her voice lowered to a provocative murmur as she traced his bottom lip with the tip of her index finger. "I like to watch, too."

He groaned and slid his hands to her hips, then thrust against her slippery heat. She'd discovered his weakness. He had an almost fetish for watching. That she had the same one had him so hard his blood surged in his ears. "Okay."

Her breathing hitched, but those eyes flashed at him, hot and amused. "You like that idea."

"Just a little." He leaned forward, brushing his mouth over hers. "Condom, babe. Back pocket of my jeans."

The little hellcat had the nerve to grin at him again and cocked a brow. "Do you always carry a condom?"

"Yes. It's always better to be prepared." He brushed his mouth over hers and skimmed his palms up her belly, cupping each breast. He made sure to flick her nipples, enough to make her breathing hitch. "I'll bet you carry them in your purse, that you were carrying some that first date at the masquerade."

"Okay, so you got me on that one." A soft blush stained her cheeks. She slid from his lap. The little minx bent straight over as she reached into his jeans pocket. After pulling out the condom, she resettled herself on his knees.

He took the condom from her and tore it open, rolling it in place, then smacked her ass. "Now stop talking and ride me, baby."

Mandy clamped a hand over her mouth, giggling behind her fingers. "That's a terrible line."

He rolled his eyes. "I'm about two seconds from tossing your shapely ass onto that bed over there. I'm slowly losing patience with this."

She stilled in his lap. Her gaze dropped as she smoothed a hand over him, her thumb idly caressing the scar on the corner of his shoulder.

"I'm sorry. You make me laugh." She shrugged, and something vulnerable moved across her features. "That's sexy to me. Most guys are all about the endgame."

He hooked two fingers beneath her chin, tilting her gaze back to him, and brushed his mouth over hers. "Climb on, angel."

She nodded and lifted herself up. Her toes barely touched the floor, though, giving her little leverage.

"Houston, we've got a problem." He grinned and scooted down in the chair. It was almost comical how much work it took, but the reward came when she slid onto him.

Mandy moaned quietly, dropped her forehead onto his shoulder and rolled her hips, then moaned again. "I always wondered what you'd feel like. It's *so* much better than the fantasy."

Only sheer force of will made him resist the near-overwhelming desire to grip her hips and satiate the need she'd sent burning through his blood. Holy mother of Christ.

She was hot and wet and tight, and she was right. In this position, he could see everything in the mirror behind her. His cock disappearing into her. The luscious curve of her ass. Even her trembling thighs.

He turned his mouth to her ear. "Go, angel. Right now, I'm beyond thought, and I don't want to hurt you, so I'm officially putting you in control of this."

She lifted her head from his shoulder, nodded, and brushed her mouth over his. Hands braced on his shoulders, she rolled her hips in slow circles. His cock moved in increments inside of her, not providing nearly enough friction, but Mandy moaned quietly, so Marcus contented himself with watching her. He slid his hands up her stomach, massaging her small, pert breasts and pinching her nipples. All the while she continued to roll her hips, grinding against him.

She attempted to rise again, but even on her tiptoes, her thrusts were shallow at best. He drew a steadying breath and forced himself to focus on her reflection in the mirror, on stroking her body. Tonight was about her. Her needs. Her pleasure. Not his.

When her movements took on an awkward jerking, Mandy growled, low and frustrated.

Unable to stand the lack of friction anymore, he gripped her hips to stop her movement. "Angel?"

Panting by this point, she went still and opened her eyes. "Hmm?"

"Is this doing anything for you?"

She bit her bottom lip, gnashing it between her teeth, then sighed and giggled. "Not nearly enough."

She pushed her toes against the floor. Or at least she tried. All she managed was the same awkward bouncing.

"Sitting on your lap like this, I can barely get enough leverage, and the thrusts are..." She let out an insane little giggle and went limp in his lap, shoulders slumping. "God, this was such a bad idea. All I'm getting is frustrated."

He chuckled and leaned forward, brushing his mouth over hers. "You get points for originality, but we're getting up, because if this continues, I'll die of frustration."

Mandy giggled again, but clamped a hand over her mouth. "I'm so sorry."

"It's okay. But we *are* getting up. Hold on." She nodded and wrapped her arms around his neck. Holding her securely by the ass, he pushed out of the chair, carried her the two steps to the bed, and set her on top. Her ass hit the edge, not nearly where he wanted to be. Some part of his brain told him he ought to lay her fully on top, to love her long and slow, but he was beyond rational thought. He braced one hand on the bed beside her hip, used his other to hook her left knee, and sank deep, then pulled out and pushed in again.

Mandy moaned, her eyes rolling closed in bliss. Her hands slid down his back to cup his ass. "*Oohhh*, this is so much better."

He heartily agreed, but his reply came out as more of a garbled grunt as pleasure shuddered through him. Holy fucking Christ. She wrapped around him like a warm, wet glove, creating the most incredible friction. He gave himself permission to relish the sensation and found a slow, deep rhythm.

Mandy uttered a litany of quiet moans and arched against

him, her hips rising to meet his. Her breathing increased, her chest heaving. Her warm, ragged breaths teased his skin. Her nails dug into his ass where she clutched at him. Every thrust propelled them faster, drove them harder.

Until all that registered were her soft mewling cries and the creak of the bed beneath them. He tried desperately to hold on to himself, but Mandy was Mandy. In the throes of passion, she was so goddamn beautiful. He couldn't stop watching the bliss travel across her features. Every gasp and sigh made his balls tighten and ache.

No. When he went, he was for damn sure taking her with him. He reached between them, found her swollen clit and flicked it with his thumb. "Come on, angel. I'm not going to come till you do."

She moaned again, hips bowing into the pressure of his finger. Rubbing circles around her clit, he pulled out until only the tip of him remained and then shoved hard into her. Mandy sucked in a sharp breath, her body going rigid beneath him. Her thighs trembled.

So he pulled out again and thrust again, sending the bed shaking and her headboard knocking the wall. She groaned, long and low. Her heat clamped around him, and she cried out, her belly trembling. She tossed her head back, body bowing off the bed, hips growing a jerky rhythm as her inner walls squeezed his cock.

Marcus swore under his breath. The sensation was too much. Like a bolt of lightning straight out of the sky, his orgasm rushed over him. Her soft cries filled his ears. Her body shook beneath him. Her perfume, that sweet vanilla, mixed with the scent of sex and *her*, filled his lungs. He trembled helplessly, the pleasure seemingly never-ending.

When the spasms finally released him, he collapsed forward, dropping his forehead onto her shoulder. "Holy shit."

He dragged in desperate breaths. Every muscle and bone in his body felt weighted by lead. He couldn't have moved if he tried. Legs still locked around his hips and panting every bit as hard as he was, Mandy simply clutched him tight. How long they stayed that way, he couldn't be sure, but eventually he found the energy to lift his head.

Her damp skin glistened in the low light of the room. Curls clung to her forehead and neck, her hair in tangled disarray around her head. Mandy grinned at him, her eyes gleaming with triumph and satiation. God, she was beautiful looking at him like that. She made him want to beat his damn chest. That look right there solidified his decision. Whatever happened when this ended, he could never be sorry for this time with her.

He brushed back a thick curl. "You look like a cat who just got away with gobbling up the family goldfish."

Mandy winked and smacked his ass. "You're not too shabby in the sack, sailor."

"Minx." He chuckled again and brushed his mouth over hers. "I'll be right back."

He eased out of her and straightened away from the bed, padding out of the room and down the hall to the bathroom. When he returned to the bedroom a couple minutes later, Mandy had slid beneath the covers and lay on her side, eyes closed. He climbed in as quietly as he could, but as he settled beside her, her eyelids fluttered open.

She gave him a soft, sleepy-eyed smile. "Hi."

He rolled onto his back and held his arm out in invitation. "Hi, yourself."

Mandy settled her head in the crook of his shoulder with a contented sigh. "Mr. Denali, I do believe you wore me out."

"Good." He chuckled. "Maybe next time we'll just go for old-fashioned and simple, huh?"

She raised a hand, waving an invisible flag, and giggled. "I bow to your experience. My assistant at work gave me the idea. She has a tendency to tell me about her and her fiancé's escapades. She said the position was awesome."

Marcus tilted his head to peer down at her. "She's taller than you, isn't she?"

Mandy nodded, then buried her face in his chest and giggled, snorted, then giggled some more. He could only stare at the textured ceiling and grin like an idiot. It had to be a bad sign, but Christ, he loved that sound.

With one last hiccup, she finally quieted, and reached up to wipe a finger beneath her eyes. "I'm sorry. I tend to get emotional after really good sex."

He chuckled. "I'll take that as a compliment."

She was quiet a moment, her fingers idly walking his belly. "Marcus?"

"Hmm?"

She slid her hand over his belly and hugged him tight. "I'm glad you came over tonight."

He wrapped both arms around her and pressed a kiss into her hair. "Me too."

Too much so. Being with her should have felt awkward,

everything given, but it didn't. Her body beside him felt as natural as breathing. It scared the living shit out of him. Mandy had his mind running in circles. Just being with her challenged every belief he'd held up until this point. Was he really happy with the road he'd set himself on all those years ago? Was he really happy living this way? Or only kidding himself?

CHAPTER EIGHT

The sight of Marcus Denali's bare ass in her bed had to rank among the top five best moments of her life. Lying on her side in the dim light of the early morning, Mandy soaked in the gorgeous body beside her. He lay on his stomach, gloriously naked, arms up around his ears. The sheets and blankets were draped low across his thighs, as if he'd gotten hot and flung them back, leaving the top half of him bare to her greedy gaze.

She gave herself a moment to enjoy the sight of all those firm muscles and his warm, satiny skin, then forced herself to get out of bed. The night had come to end. All too soon he'd have to leave, and the last place she wanted to be was naked beside him when it happened.

If she was going to survive this month playing his girlfriend, she needed to separate herself from the sex. She needed to remember this was only a fling, her chance to fulfill a fantasy. Anything more would be squashed.

Which meant she was getting up and getting moving. Coffee first, then a shower and work. She had a meeting with a new client at nine and lunch with Steph at noon to discuss ideas for her wedding dress. She'd wake Marcus after she made the coffee.

After finding and pulling on last night's discarded T-shirt and panties, she headed for the kitchen. There, she brewed a pot of coffee and waited for it to finish. Just as she was pouring her first cup, the soft padding of footsteps came up the hallway. Cup in hand, she turned in time to watch a fully dressed Marcus stop in the entrance.

Tension rose over the small space like a living, breathing entity. Her insides shook. Here came the awkward morning-after routine. What the hell did she say? Thanks for a great time? They all ended the same way. An excuse, a sweet kiss, a hasty good-bye. Then the guy would rush out the door. All while she ignored the emptiness she felt inside.

She smiled and clutched her mug tightly, praying he couldn't see her trembling hands. "Morning."

"Morning." He stuffed his hands in his pockets and returned a polite, if not a tad uncomfortable, smile.

She lifted her mug in his direction and raised her brows. "Would you like some?"

"Please." He nodded and moved to lean against the counter beside her. His scent swirled around her, all warm, sleepy male and something earthy, with a hint of engine grease, making her knees wobble. God, why was it that smell melted her insides?

She pulled down a mug from the cabinet and filled it before glancing back at him. "How do you take it?"

He flashed another tight, polite smile. "Cream and sugar if you have it."

She nodded and turned to the cabinets, getting down the plastic container she kept the sugar in. "I'm afraid I don't have creamer, though. I take mine black. All I have is milk."

"That'll do."

She nodded again and moved to the fridge, got out the jug of milk and set it on the counter beside the sugar.

"Thanks." Marcus caught her gaze and smiled—again—before turning to the mug on the counter.

"Yup." The tension pervading the room grated on already raw nerves. It was so thick she could cut it up and serve it to him. If something didn't give soon, she'd go insane.

Marcus dumped two teaspoons of sugar and a healthy pour of milk into his mug. She grinned. "I didn't take you as a girly coffee drinker."

A more natural grin appeared on his face as he stirred his coffee. "I have a sweet tooth, so sue me." He looked over at her as he sipped his coffee. "We'll get used to each other."

Mandy blew out a relieved breath, her shoulders rolling forward as the tension finally released her. "I hope so. I hate this part."

"Me too." He studied her a moment, then set his mug on the counter behind him and turned to her. So close now the warmth of his body infused hers, he cupped her face in his palms and pressed a tender kiss to her lips once, twice. Then he tucked a lock of hair behind her ear with the tip of his index finger. "Hi."

Thank goodness for the solidity of the counter behind her,

because every bone liquefied. She could not handle it when he went all sweet on her. It had that romantic girl inside of her, the one who totally geeked out at planning beautiful, fantasy weddings every day, dreaming of *what if*.

She sighed, her body sagging into his. Yeah, she was so toast. "Hi."

He thumbed her chin. "I'm sorry I have to leave so early. Gram goes to church Sunday mornings, and I left Cammie with her last night. I need to go pick her up. She doesn't like to be left alone."

Mandy raised her brows. "Cammie. Your dog?"

He nodded.

"Cute name." She smiled. "You named her after camouflage, I assume?"

One corner of his mouth hitched and Marcus shrugged. "Her coloring reminded me of it. You'll see when you meet her. You'll like her. She loves everybody." He laughed quietly and turned to pick up his coffee off the counter, sipping at it before he spoke again. "Definitely not a good watch dog."

"Like Trent and Lauren's new dog, Bo." Mandy laughed, picturing her brother's new German shepherd. "He's an eighty-pound meathead. He barks at the leaves blowing in the trees outside but greets everybody with slobbery kisses and a wagging behind."

"You know." Marcus glanced at her as he sipped his coffee. "This would be a lot easier if you stayed at my place. I've got a built-in doggie door, so Cammie can let herself out in the mornings. Then we wouldn't be so rushed. You wanted nights, right?"

She looked up at him and shrugged. "Yes."

He leaned into her, body heat enveloping her, and lowered his voice. "Me too. I told you. Casual flings with strangers don't do it for me anymore."

"But you don't want commitment." She pursed her lips and shook her head. "Isn't that a bit mixed up?"

He huffed a laugh. "Yeah, I guess it is. I'm human, sweetheart, like everyone else."

It was that human side, the heart of the man she caught sight of on occasion, that always had her dreaming of *what if*. She'd bet every last cent she had that when it came right down to it, he'd make some woman very happy someday. And damned if the thought didn't have the green-eyed monster growling in her head.

She flashed her brightest smile and winked, determined to cover the possessiveness suddenly rolling through her. "Then I guess it's a good thing I'm not fond of robots."

He stared at her for a beat, something somber moving across the recesses of his eyes, there long enough that she could see it but completely untouchable. It wasn't the first time she'd seen the look or ones like it. She was dying to ask what was on his mind, but would he even tell her? Then again, maybe it was better if he didn't. The less she knew about him, the less involved she became and the more of her heart she kept to herself.

Before she could think of what *to* say, he glanced at the stove and frowned.

"Shoot. I should go." He set his coffee on the counter and edged closer, leaning into her and brushing his mouth over hers. Soft and sweet, he lingered for a moment, his kiss so unlike the man who'd drawn firm boundaries on their relationship.

When she was lost in him all over again, he finally pulled back. He stroked a stray curl out of her eyes. "I'll call you later. I'd like to introduce you to my grandmother sometime this week, but I'll need to talk to her first."

The reminder of her place in his life had disappointment tightening her chest and weighting her limbs. Mandy forced a smile and nodded. "Sounds good."

Marcus pressed another kiss to her mouth, this one so tender her insides melted. "Talk to you later."

He smiled, soft and full of promise, then pivoted and left the room. As the front door closed behind him with a quiet snap, determination swelled behind her breastbone. She needed to stop allowing these fanciful notions to creep into her head, to stop allowing herself to get so caught up in *him*. At the end of the day, she knew where this led. Nowheresville.

No, she needed to focus on the sex. She and Marcus had agreed to play out each other's fantasies. So that's what she'd concentrate on...a way to surprise him the next time they got together.

* * *

The conversation around him faded to a muted hum as Marcus stared at his phone. He was seated at one of two picnic tables set up behind the shop, the guys around him all chatting while wolfing down mouthfuls of the sandwiches Lauren had brought down earlier. Mandy's text had arrived a few seconds ago. It had only been two days since he last saw her, but he hadn't stopped craving her since. Or looking forward to the next time he'd see her. Her text was short and sweet, but like the woman, it teased his senses.

It's your turn.

He ought to put his phone away and concentrate on the men around him. They had a bike to finish restoring, an old Harley, and the owner wanted it finished for an auction next week. They still had a lot of details to go over. But a few simple words from Mandy pulled his thoughts from where they ought to be and cranked his desire to a low boil.

He shouldn't have suggested she start staying at his place. Hell, he shouldn't have agreed to this whole month-long fling in the first place, but he wasn't sorry for it. Lying in her arms, talking, laughing...She filled something within him he hadn't realized was missing. It left him all too aware how lonely his life had become. He went to work, took care of his grandmother, and came home to his dog. Occasionally, he and the guys went out for a beer, but most nights he fell asleep watching the news, Cammie curled up on his lap. A simple, uncomplicated life.

And an empty one.

Mandy offered the opposite. She had a smile for everyone, and not a whole lot bothered her. He envied her carefree manner. She grabbed life by its ears.

He read her text again and typed out a quick response. *My turn for what?*

The more of her he got, the more he wanted. Just the thought of her had his pulse pounding and his cock stirring in his jeans. He couldn't wait to see her again.

Her reply came almost instantly.

We're playing out fantasies, correct?

Damn. She had to go and say that. And here he was sitting across the table from her brother. Not that he had the power to deny her.

Well, the whole idea was I'd help you fulfill yours...

Barely ten seconds passed before her reply popped up.

Nope. It's mutual or nothing. Not fair if u get nothing out of this.

Marcus shook his head. Being Tuesday, chances were, she was at work. Clearly she was doing exactly what he was—sitting somewhere, probably trying to wolf down lunch, and waiting on texts from him. All of which did nothing to decrease the ache behind his zipper.

I do get something out of this—you.

Her next message came with an emoticon, a little smiley face rolling its eyes. God, he could almost see her doing it. She did it often and damned if it didn't make him smile every time.

Good. ;) Now...favorite fantasy, plz.

The back of his neck prickled. Marcus lifted his gaze from his phone and glanced around the table. Trent and Mike, seated at the left end, were discussing the paint job on the Harley. Gabe, however, sat chewing his turkey on rye, watching Marcus with an amused gleam in his eye.

Gabe swallowed and picked up his can of Coke. "We boring you?"

Marcus hastily set his phone on the table. Shit. He felt like a horny kid caught sexting. "Gram. Wants me to pick up milk on the way home."

"Uh-huh." Gabe's mouth hitched as he took another bite of his sandwich. "Tell her I said hey."

"Yup." Marcus frowned, shook his head, and looked down at his phone. It was time to end this insanity. They were going to have to set some ground rules. Namely, no texting at work.

His hands shook as he shot off a reply. *Can't talk now. At lunch w/ the guys. I'll call you later.*

He locked his screen and returned his phone to his back pocket. When he finally looked up again, all three men were staring at him. Gabe was still chewing that damn sandwich and watching him. Trent, seated beside Gabe, stared at him with a full-out, shit-eating grin. Marcus's stomach tightened. Shit, shit, shit. It was one thing for Trent to know he and Mandy had been set up together through Military Match, or hell, even to know he was attracted to her at all.

Their fling was something else entirely, and that was a conversation he had no desire to have with her brother.

Mike glanced over at Marcus, and a slow grin stretched across his face. "Was that the one from Military Match?"

"Yup." Marcus stood, climbed over the table's bench seat, and picked up his plate, taking his half-eaten sandwich with him. "And that's all the details you're getting. I'm going back to work. We've only got five days to finish this thing and too damn much still to do."

"Ah, come on. At least tell me if you're seeing her again,"

Mike called out behind him as Marcus reached the back door.

"Oh, I'm betting he'll be seeing her again." This from Trent, whose voice filled with amusement.

"How the hell do you know that?" Mike asked.

Marcus stormed into the workshop, leaving behind the laughter and murmurs erupting in his wake. The whole damn notion of being discussed over lunch had his stomach tied in sickening knots. Trent seemed okay with the knowledge that he and Mandy were together, but would he feel the same knowing they were essentially using each other?

The whole notion left a sour taste in his mouth. She deserved better than him. If he was smart, he'd go back to Military Match and have Karen set him up with someone else.

* * *

The chime on the front door rang through the speaker fed into the workshop. Marcus lifted his head from the clutch he was assembling and glanced through the doorway leading to the front of the shop. His heart stalled, then took off at a sprint. Shit. Mandy. Wearing a tight white blouse and an equally tight pencil skirt, she sauntered to the front counter and leaned on the top. She banged the bell and turned her head her as if in search of someone. When her gaze finally landed on him, a slow, sexy smile curled across her face, making his cock twitch. He pushed onto his feet and followed her siren's call.

Heart hammering from the vicinity of his tonsils, he

grabbed a rag from a nearby table, wiping his hands as he headed for the front of the shop.

"I got it," he called out to the room at large.

When he finally reached the counter, he set his hands firmly on top. It took every ounce of self-control he had not to wrap himself around her. "What are you doing here?"

Still grinning like the cat who'd eaten the family parakeet, she held out her hand. "Key. Since you aren't answering my texts, I guess I'm going to have to take matters into my own hands."

His cock twitched again, already lengthening against his zipper. He hadn't a clue what she meant, but he'd happily follow if she'd only keep looking at him like she wanted to eat *him* for dinner. "Key for what?"

She rolled her eyes. "Your house. My last appointment is at three. I thought I'd use it to my advantage. I've decided I don't want to wait until this weekend to see you again, so I'm kidnapping you for the night."

Marcus swallowed hard. Christ. Did she have any idea how sexy this take-no-prisoners attitude of hers was?

She *tsk*ed and moved around the counter, stopping so close her soft vanilla scent floated around him, and her warm breaths teased his lips. Holding his gaze with a boldness that dared him to deny her, she shoved her hand in his left pocket. "Guess I'll have to get them myself."

Her fingers grazed his quickly awakening cock, and Marcus squeezed his eyes shut. He gritted his teeth, holding on to what little sanity he still had. "Jesus, Mandy."

She pulled his keys from his pocket. The sound of jingling metal filled the silence. "This one?"

At her question, he opened his eyes, then forced himself to take a step back. *Focus, Denali.* "What do you need it for?"

"You'll see." She winked and held up another key from the ring. "This one?"

He took the keys from her hand. The sooner he gave her what she wanted, the sooner she'd leave. Before the guys caught them together. Or he did something he'd regret. Like pull her into the office, close the door, and find out whether or not she was wearing panties beneath that ass-hugging skirt of hers.

He pulled off his house key, then jotted down his address on the notepad near the register and handed both to her. "It's not far. Now, what—"

"Thanks." She snatched the key and note, leaned in, and pecked his cheek, but paused there, her voice lowering to a husky murmur. "You won't regret it."

She had the nerve to flick her tongue against his earlobe, then pivoted and strode toward the front door, once again leaving him to watch her sashaying ass as she walked away from him.

"Oh, I almost forgot." She paused at the door and looked back. "Your dog won't bite, will she?"

As tongue-tied as he'd been the first time he'd asked a girl on a damn date, he could only shake his head.

"Didn't think so, but figured I should ask. See you later, Marcus." She tossed a wave behind her as she pulled open the front door and strode out.

He watched until she climbed into her car, then turned to head to the back again, only to come up short. The guys all stood in the doorway. Gabe had his arms folded, one dark brow cocked. Trent had an arm slung over Gabe's shoulder. Both men grinned. Damn it. Mike stared, wide-eyed and slack-jawed, in the direction of the front door.

Marcus's stomach tightened. The jig was up.

He shot a glare between the three of them and pushed into the workshop behind them. "All right, all right. Show's over. We've got a restoration to complete."

CHAPTER NINE

Mandy tipped her head back, taking in the one-level house in front of her. For some reason, she'd figured a guy who rode a hog and wore a leather jacket would live in a cramped, messy one-bedroom apartment. Instead, Marcus lived in a small, residential neighborhood, one of the housing developments that had begun cropping up all over the place in the last few years. The kind full of families.

Container of cookies clutched under one arm, she climbed the front porch steps and shoved the key into the door, anxiety twisting in her stomach. If she was going to keep her head in the game, she needed a target, hence her decision to surprise him with something sexy. Of course, if she was honest with herself, she'd admit she'd merely dreamed up a reason to see him. It wasn't even the weekend.

She would most definitely not ponder how good it had felt to lie in his arms. Or how tender and generous he was in bed, making her wonder why she'd ever settled for one-night stands with clumsy, drunken lovers in the first place. Or even how confident he made her feel. Tonight's outfit was not something she'd normally have picked out for herself. No, she'd have put on something that accentuated her breasts and disguised her bottom half.

And she was only wearing it for one reason: because she couldn't wait to see Marcus's face when he saw her in it.

So she was forcing herself to concentrate on the phenomenal sex. If she only had a month with him, then she was for darned sure getting her fill of him and his expert hands.

She pushed open the door. As she stepped inside, a small dog came running out from the back of the house, her tail wagging with excitement. As her gaze landed on Mandy, she skittered off into the living room and began to bark.

All thoughts of her sexy little plan went *POOF!*

"You must be Cammie."

The small dog inched her way back into the foyer, barking the whole way.

Mandy released the doorknob and laughed softly. She squatted, setting the container on the floor at her feet, and stretched a hand in the dog's direction. "I have to admit, you're not at all what I expected. I expected you to be some huge Rottweiler or a Doberman. You couldn't possibly weigh more than ten pounds."

Cammie halted several feet from her and barked again, this one with enough force her tiny front feet left the ground. A tail that resembled a question mark continued to wag, and the dog crept forward, alternating between sniffing the air and barking some more. Mandy stretched further, attempting to stroke the dog's head, but Cammie took off into the living room again.

"Come on, sweetie. I won't bite." Mandy wiggled her fingers. When Ferocious peeked around the tan leather sofa but refused to budge, Mandy rested her elbows on her knees. "At some point we're going to have to make friends because, like it or not, I'm coming in."

Bark!

Okay, so she really was adorable. She resembled the Chihuahua one of her clients had brought to a meeting once, with the small head, long legs, and big black eyes that seemed to bug out of her head. She had unusual markings though, brown fur with black stripes, no doubt the inspiration for her name.

Mandy popped the top of the container, which held dog biscuits she'd purchased at Lauren's bakery, and held out the treat. "Do you like cookies?"

The barking immediately stopped and the little head cocked sideways, ears shooting straight up.

"Yeah, I thought you might. Bo insists these things are better than kibble." She laughed softly and wiggled the treat. "You'll have to come and get it, though."

The dog stepped forward slowly and sniffed the air again. She stopped a few feet away, then reached out and took the cookie carefully, all the while watching Mandy with wary eyes. As the dog concentrated on gobbling up her treat, Mandy took the chance to make friends and stroked the little head. "Okay, so he's right. You are the sweetest little thing."

When the cookie was gone, Cammie promptly sat and pawed at Mandy's hand.

"Now that we're proper friends"—Mandy stroked Cammie's head and the crooked little tail wagged—"how 'bout you show me around this place, huh? Then you can help me get ready. He'll be home in about two hours, and I have a lot to do."

* * *

Marcus set down the chopper's kickstand and shut off the engine, but he couldn't force himself to get off the bike. He stared at the crotch rocket parked a few feet beyond him in the driveway. Of course Mandy would choose a sport bike over a hog, and bright red to boot, to match her car and her carefree attitude.

Just the sight of that bike made his heart heavy. He hadn't stopped thinking about her since the phone call he'd received two hours ago. Jason, the young soldier who'd just joined his veterans support group, had committed suicide this morning. His wife had found Marcus's number in the young man's phone. Marcus had given it to the guy his first night in group. All members exchanged numbers, so they'd have someone to call if they were having trouble coping.

And like every other time, talking to a family member whose world had just imploded had sent his mind on a spiral straight to hell. It had gone a little too much like the phone call he'd gotten from Gram after Ava's suicide.

Now, the sight of Mandy's bike in his driveway filled him with a yearning that made his gut ache. Guilt was eating him alive. What he desperately needed tonight was a distraction, and Mandy provided a lure he wasn't sure he could resist. God knew she'd be the perfect thing to lose himself and his grief in, but it would feel like he was using her, because he'd be doing it for all the wrong reasons.

With a heavy sigh, he forced himself to get off the bike and go inside. When he pushed open the front door, Cammie came rushing out from the kitchen, her nails dancing over the hardwood floor as she pranced around him, begging for attention. When he didn't pet her right away, she stretched her front paws up his right leg. Some part of his brain told him to at least bend down and greet her, but the sultry singing drifting from farther inside the house caught him. Mandy sung upbeat lyrics to a song he couldn't hear. The mere sound of her voice was enough to send need winding through him all over again.

He dropped his gaze to Cammie instead and stroked the dog's head. "Hey there, girl. Sounds like we have company."

She wagged her tail.

"Come on. Let's go say hello." He followed Mandy's voice into the kitchen and stopped in the entrance, caught by the sight of her. She stood at the sink at the far end with her back to him, washing dishes, her shapely ass swaying to the tune she now hummed.

In tight black leather pants that hugged every gorgeous curve and a matching jacket that showed off her midriff, she looked...edible. That and the containers lining the stove told him she'd gone through a lot of trouble for him tonight. And in about two seconds he was going to let her down and send her home.

Mandy shut off the water and reached for a towel on the counter. When her gaze landed on him, she jumped.

"You're home." She held her arms out from her sides and turned a slow circle, tossing a sultry smile over her shoulder. The heat in her eyes when she finally faced him again burned him up from the inside out. "What do you think?"

Oh, the outfit was sexy as hell. Any other day, he'd enjoy peeling her out of all that leather. Tonight, all he could think about was that poor kid and his wife, left to pick up the pieces.

He forced himself to turn away from her. "You should go. It's been a hell of a day. I'm sorry you went through all the trouble, but I'm not fit for company tonight."

He focused on putting one foot in front of the other as he made his way to the back of the house, Cammie on his heels. Upon reaching his bedroom, he stripped off his T-shirt, covered in a mixture of oil and gasoline, and hurled it in the direction of the hamper, seated along the far wall. It landed in a ball on the floor three feet from his target. If that didn't just sum up his whole damn day.

"You okay?"

The sound of Mandy's voice, soft with concern, slid along every aching nerve ending. A siren's song, so hard to resist that if he looked at her, he'd give in to the pull.

Frustration owned him right now, though. If he gave in to her, he'd probably use her like a ten-dollar hooker. And she'd probably let him, but she deserved better. So much better. Shit. He was a selfish ass.

"Marcus, talk to me." This time, her voice came as a quiet plea, calling to him as he popped the button of his jeans free.

Thoughts of Ava swirled in his head, combined with memories of his young friend, all of it whirling around him, pulling him off-balance. He closed his eyes and drew a breath to the count of three, then blew it out to the count of three. It was a trick he'd learned in therapy. When memories of the war threatened to suck him back, he was to take slow, deep breaths and focus on the room around him, ground himself in reality. It worked nearly every time.

This time, he couldn't relax. Every muscle in his body tensed with the effort it took not to turn and wrap himself around Mandy, for the bliss he'd find in her arms. "It's been a bad day, and I'm not myself tonight."

He crossed to the dresser, yanked open the drawer with all the frustration winding through him, pulled out a clean T-shirt, and slammed the drawer shut again. Death was a part of life. On some plane of existence, he knew that, understood it, but he'd seen too damn much. Lost one too many people. At the end of their month, he'd lose Mandy, too. The thought had his heart in a knot in his chest, and if he let himself need her, that's exactly what would happen.

No, what he needed to do was put some distance between them. Reset those damn boundaries.

A warm, soft hand touched his back, and Marcus flinched. "Let me help."

He fisted his hands. "Mandy, in about two seconds I'm going to do something I know I'll regret."

He'd pin her to that wall beside her and fuck her until he couldn't think anymore. Until the demons curling through his skull finally eased. It wouldn't be slow or sweet, either.

Mandy slid her hands around his rib cage and up his chest, pressing her cheek into his back. "I'm not afraid of you."

He dropped the clothing onto the bed, pulled her hands free, and turned, backing her against the wall beside the bedroom door. He set his hands on either side of her head and leaned in close, only just managing to resist the urge to seize her mouth and kiss her breathless. "New rules."

Mandy blinked, stared wide-eyed for a moment, then straightened her shoulders. "Okay."

"No surprising me at the shop. Consider this Vegas. What happens here"—he waved a finger between them—"stays here. I got all kinds of shit today for that little stunt you pulled this afternoon. I'm a private person, and the last thing I want or need is to wave this under your brother's nose."

Her lips parted, and Mandy nodded slowly. "Ahhh, so that's what's got you so hot under the collar. I surprised you at the shop and you haven't told Trent we're seeing each other. I'm—"

"We're not seeing each other, Mandy. We're sleeping together. There's a huge difference." He pivoted away from her and paced toward the bed. "The guys are asking questions, and I don't know what the hell to tell them. I sure as hell don't want to have to be the one to explain to your brother that I'm screwing his sister."

Mandy remained silent behind him. For too damn long. He hated himself for saying that to her, but it was the truth. He was keeping a secret from one of his closest friends. The whole notion made him sick to his stomach. Would Trent still tease him if he knew their arrangement? That it was all about sex and he and Mandy weren't supposed to see each other again once the month was over?

"You know," Mandy said, a hard, determined edge to her voice, "I'm not sure what the hell happened between when I saw you this afternoon and now, but I'm not going anywhere. I can see something is wrong, so until you tell me what the hell is going on, I'm afraid you're stuck with me."

Marcus halted mid-stride, and just that fast, with a few harsh words from one of the most stubborn women he'd ever met, all the fight drained out of him. She had to go and say that. Remind him. Stand in front of him and refuse to let him run. When Trent had come home from his last tour she'd done the same thing for him. She'd taken care of him, despite being told more than once it wasn't wanted, and had enlisted Lauren's help. Now here she was, storming her way into Marcus's own version of hell.

God, she had guts. How could he be angry at her for having courage when he didn't?

He closed his eyes, his shoulders heavy as defeat crept over him. "How is it you're even still here?"

"Is that what you were doing? Trying to get me to leave?"

He forced himself to face her. She deserved that much, and hell, at this point, he had nothing left. He was baring his belly, every raw nerve open and exposed and at her mercy. "Yes. I need you tonight. But it's a completely selfish need. I got bad news this afternoon, and it's got my head going to bad places. The only thing I could think about all the way here was you. Knowing you'd be here waiting. But I don't have a right to ask that from you."

"You're too serious for your own good, you know that? I'm not going anywhere. You need me? I'm here." She laid a hand against his chest. "What do you need?"

"A fifth of scotch? A punching bag? You? Hell. I don't know." He glanced down at himself. "I need a shower, though. Fuel system on the bike we're working on sprang a leak."

Mandy wrinkled her nose. "I can tell."

He shook his head slowly, dejection weighing him down. "And yet you're still here."

"You forget. I do my own car repairs. I happen to like the smell of engine on a man. Just maybe not quite so much of it." Mandy laughed softly and slipped her hand into his, tugging him behind her as she headed for the attached bathroom. "How 'bout we start with a bath? I did a little snooping while I waited for you to get home. You have a gorgeous tub that's been calling my name."

* * *

Twenty minutes later, he and Mandy sat in the two-person tub in the master bathroom. She sat behind him, her supple thighs on either side of his hips. Her breasts pressed against his back as she leaned over his shoulder, slowly moving a soapy washcloth across his chest.

He dropped his head back against her shoulder. The tension that had caged his chest when he'd walked in the door had long since evaporated. His muscles were so relaxed his limbs were as limp as cooked noodles. Some part of him insisted it was childish to let her wash him, that he ought to be doing this for *her*, but he couldn't resist if he tried. The simple warmth of her body against his back soothed the ache in his chest.

He slid his hand up her arm, her skin warm and slick beneath his fingers. "Thanks."

She leaned her cheek against his, her voice low and soft. "For what?"

"This." He captured her hand, wrapping his fingers around hers. "It's nice."

"You say that like you've never taken a bath with a woman before."

The tease in her voice pulled a quiet chuckle out of him. "I haven't."

"Never had sex in a public place, haven't taken a bath with a woman." She *tsk*ed and set the washcloth moving again, this time toward his belly. "Where have you been, Marcus?"

"Living under a rock, apparently."

She nipped at his jaw, her voice low, sexy, husky. "Well, we're going to have to fix that."

He turned his head and leaned back enough to see her face. "Is that so?"

He expected some sort of sassy comeback, but her hand paused beneath the water, and her expression sobered. She studied him for a long moment, then touched his cheek. "Tell me."

He sighed and straightened, focused his gaze on the frosted window covering the wall opposite the tub. He couldn't look in her eyes when he said the words. She'd strip him bare in two seconds flat. "Got a phone call this afternoon, not long after you left. One of the guys in my support group committed suicide this morning. His name was Jason. He was new to the group and just off a deployment. His wife called me. She found him in the upstairs bathroom. In the tub of all damn things."

Mandy drew a sharp breath. "Oh my God. His poor wife. Did you know him well?"

"Just from group. He was army and much younger than me. Barely twenty-five." He sat silent a moment, idly walking his fingers over the skin on her forearm. He owed it to her to tell her the truth, but he wasn't sure he could get the words out. "There's more."

"I kind of figured there was." Mandy rested her chin on his shoulder again, her voice lowering to a murmur. "You don't have to tell me."

"Mmm. But you've been very patient with me."

"That's what friends do, right? We care for each other when needed and don't ask questions."

"Is that what we are? Friends?" He repeated the word, tasted the flavor of it on his tongue. Why did it sound all wrong coming from her? That had been his rule when they'd made this damn agreement in the first place. Now? He didn't know if he could ever consider her only a friend. He wanted her too much.

She went silent, so still behind him even her breathing seemed to pause, and he could almost hear the things she wasn't saying. He couldn't be sure if he wanted her to voice them or not. He'd opened a can of worms, and some part of him insisted it shouldn't bother him.

Finally, she picked up the washcloth again, rewashing his shoulders this time. "No. We're lovers. But the idea is the same."

He grunted. Something deep in his gut rebelled against the idea. She'd been his lover for what, two days? A week? Hell, at this point, he'd lost track. All he knew was that the word "friends" left a bitter taste on his tongue. Friends meant she'd go back to dating other men. Just the idea made him want to put his fist through something.

He shoved the thoughts away—the same way he always did—and forced himself to focus on what he *could* have with her. If he truly wanted a friend when this was over, he'd have to learn to talk to her. The problem was, spilling his guts didn't come easy or natural.

He drew a deep breath and blew it out, releasing pent-up emotion along with it. "I suppose I owe you the truth. Why my friend's death bothers me so much, I mean."

"You don't owe me anything." Her voice came warm and soft in his ear, lacking the judgment he'd expected.

He squeezed her fingers in a vain attempt to tell her what he couldn't find the words to say. "It's just...not easy to talk about."

"Never was for Trent, either, but I'm here if you need someone to listen."

He appreciated that. More than he could tell her.

He focused on the feel of her hand in his, on her body against his back, and let her presence soothe the wound itself. He needed that connection. Not to anyone. To her. There was something about her that calmed the storm raging through him. "If you took a tour of the house, then I assume you've seen the pictures?"

The washcloth paused on a stroke across his chest. "The girl? Yes. You have a lot of her. Who is she?"

"My sister, Ava." God, just saying her name hurt. Four years had passed, but the wound was still fresh.

"She looks nothing like you."

He gave a bitter laugh. Ava had been a dark blonde with bright blue eyes that always seemed to laugh at him. "No. She got her looks from Mom. I took after Dad. We were like night and day."

Ava had always told him he was too serious, that he needed to lighten up a little. At least she had when she was in a manic phase. Ava had been like a bouncy ball in a small room, bright and fun and filled with energy. When the depression hit, though, it snuffed that light like someone had flipped a switch.

Mandy went still again behind him, only her breathing in his ear for a moment. "Something happened to her."

"She died." The memory of the phone call he'd received four years ago rose in his mind, and his chest tightened. "She committed suicide. Swallowed a bottle of prescription pills."

"And your friend's death reminds you of it." Her arms released his shoulders only to wrap around his rib cage. Her legs tightened around his waist. "I'm so sorry. Who found her?"

For a moment, Marcus sat in stunned silence. She'd essentially wrapped her entire body around his back, and despite the warm water, it was *her* warmth that suffused him. Every breath he drew filled his lungs with the scent of soap and her, drawing him from the painful memories. He hadn't a fucking clue how to tell her what that meant. So he set his arms over hers and held on tight.

"Gram. I was in Afghanistan. My last deployment. I'd been over there for six months when she called to tell me." He'd never forget that conversation as long as he lived. Gram was one of the strongest women he knew, softhearted but formidable, but that day, she'd crumbled. "I should have been there for Ava. That was my job. To take care of her."

"It wasn't your fault." She tilted her head, her breath warm, voice low and soothing in his ear. "You go where you're told to go."

The guilt washed over him, tightening in his chest. "I volunteered. I'd been home for eighteen months, and I wanted to be back out there. There was a unit shipping out soon, and I needed a break. I loved Ava, but she was exhausting. She was bipolar, but she had a tendency to decide she didn't need her meds anymore and would stop taking them. It was hard to get her to understand that she felt fine *because* of the medication. If she hit a depressive episode, she talked about suicide a lot, so she needed to be watched."

Just like a child needing supervision. It was how he knew he'd never make anyone a good father. He'd lacked the patience Ava had needed.

Mandy hugged him. "Did she go off her meds while you were overseas?"

Guilt shuddered through him, catching in his suddenly full throat. He squeezed his eyes shut for a moment, desperate to keep the wayward emotions at bay. When he was sure he

could speak again without sounding like a goddamn blub-
bering idiot, he opened his eyes and drew a cleansing breath.
"When I volunteered, she was taking her meds, seeing her
therapist. Things were good. I should never have gone."

As abruptly as she'd wrapped herself around him, Mandy
released him. She braced her hands on the side of the tub and
stood.

"Come on. We're getting out of this tub." She stepped out
onto the floor mat and faced him. Buck naked and dripping,
she held out a hand. When all he could do was watch the water drip off her nipples and slide down her belly, she wiggled
her fingers. "Come on, sailor. Get your ass up."

He couldn't help his smile. God, he loved it when she was
bossy. That impish glint in her eyes drew him out of the shit
raging in his head.

He took her hand and let her pull him onto his feet.
"Where're we going, angel?"

Because right then, he'd follow her anywhere. She was the
sun and he desperately needed her light.

She handed him a towel and smiled, eyes soft, skin glisten-
ing in the low light of the room. "My mother always insisted
a full belly was the first step to solving anything. I brought
dinner. I thought maybe we'd take it to Chism Park. We
could take Cammie. She could get a nice walk. We could have
a picnic by the water..."

Marcus shook his head as he took the towel from her and
wrapped it around his hips. "I'm touched, but you really don't
have to go through the trouble. You being here is enough."

"I know. It was supposed to be a surprise." She cocked a

brow, that sassy glint lighting in her eyes again as she picked up a second towel and wrapped it around herself. "I had plans to seduce you."

He chuckled. She really had no idea. "Angel, all you have to do is show up."

A smile bloomed in her face, tender, alluring. "Good to know, but I'd imagine you're not much in the mood for that tonight."

She was wrong on all fronts. His whole body buzzed with the need to drown in her. He'd love nothing more than to let her seduce him, but he wouldn't use her that way. He wasn't really in the mood to be in public, either, but she'd gone through the trouble and going out would serve as a much-needed distraction.

He smiled. "Sounds great."

CHAPTER TEN

Mandy turned away from her view of Lake Washington and laid her head on Marcus's chest, listening to the soothing thump of his heartbeat. He lay on the blanket beside her with one arm tucked behind his head as he stared up at the dusky sky above them. Cammie napped contently at their feet.

They'd been at Chism Park for two hours now. While making idle chitchat, they'd polished off roast beef sandwiches served with thick hunks of cheese and fresh fruit. Cammie, she'd noted, had sat at attention beside him the entire time, though she'd quickly discovered why. Whether he did it consciously or not, Marcus would take a bite of food and then hold out some for Cammie to gobble up. It told her Cammie wasn't simply a pet to him but a companion, and that he had a kind heart. A guy who was good to animals was sexy in her book.

After they'd eaten, they'd taken the dog for a walk around the lake. The night was beautiful, clear but cool, allowing a few stars to peek through the patches of clouds. Somewhere during the walk, Marcus retreated into himself again. He'd taken her hand, threading their fingers, but went silent. She'd watched Trent do it enough over the years to recognize it and simply let him have his space.

Now, half an hour later, he had yet to say much of anything. It gave her too much time to think. Being with him this way, allowing herself to get close to him beyond the bedroom when their relationship was destined to end, was dangerous at best. But how could she turn her back on him when he clearly needed someone?

Determined to draw him out of himself, she tilted her head and stroked his chin with her fingers. "Tell me about her. Your sister, I mean."

Marcus glanced down at her and stared for a moment, eyes searching, as if perhaps she'd caught him off guard. A heartbeat later, his arm came around her, his warm palm settling on her lower back. "I'm sorry. I'm not such great company tonight."

She caressed the side of his face and lifted her head enough to smile at him. "It's okay. You don't have to tell me if you don't want to. Lauren said it always helped Trent, when she could get him to talk."

He blew out a heavy breath, his voice quiet in the evening air. "I miss her."

"I'd imagine you would. I don't know what we would've done if Trent had died over in Iraq. Dad was disappointed when Will didn't want to enlist, but Mom was glad. It meant he came home safe every night. I thought about it, enlisting, because I wanted to be like my father."

His head turned, his gaze burning into her. "Why didn't you?"

She shrugged but couldn't force herself to look at him. She was sharing things she probably shouldn't, that had old insecurities rising from the dead. If her tomboy tendencies bothered him, she didn't think she could handle seeing the disappointment in his eyes.

"Because the last thing I wanted was to be any more masculine than I already was. Growing up with brothers, with Dad, I'd always been more comfortable around men. Because of it, I had a hard time feeling feminine. Guys were..." She sighed. How did she put this in a way that didn't sound pathetic? "Let's just say it doesn't get you a lot of dates when you can kick a guy's ass in football. I would've joined a team if there'd been one, and I got called names a lot. But what I wanted, deep down, was to be more like the popular girls. Soft. Feminine. Pretty. Since clearly modeling was out—"

"Don't do that."

The gruffness of his tone stopped her rambling in its tracks. She jerked her head up to find him staring at her, brows furrowed, eyes stern.

"There's nothing wrong with you. I know a lot of guys who'd kill for a girlfriend willing to sit in the garage with them or not complain about football on Sundays."

"Yeah? Know where I can find a guy like that? 'Cause they're not exactly beating down my door." She quirked a brow, tossing his challenge back at him. He had a point, but this whole conversation dug into all those raw places. The self-doubt. The one too many men who were either turned off by her or invited her over to watch the game on Sunday. It had taken her years to realize that when they invited her over, it wasn't because they hoped to get her naked.

Marcus went silent for a moment and his body went rigid. Tension filled the air between them until it all but crackled and snapped. Mandy's stomach knotted as she waited for the fallout of her little confession.

"Me." Spoken so low she couldn't be sure she'd really heard him.

Heart now hammering her rib cage, she sat up, turning her gaze to the water, and wrapped her arms around her knees. Took a moment to put a lid back on the romantic notions bubbling in her chest.

"I told you. You in a pair of jeans covered in grease is a thing of fantasies. Believe me, that first day we met, when you barreled into me, I noticed you." Marcus followed her up and leaned his head over her shoulder, his body warm against her back. His voice came as a low hum in her ear. "You were wearing a white T-shirt covered in oil stains and a pair of jeans that hugged your fantastic ass."

She laughed. "You are so full of it. I've heard about the women you date, Marcus."

According to a conversation she'd overheard between Marcus and Trent, Marcus preferred blondes with big boobs and legs for miles. Everything she wasn't. And if she let herself ponder that, she'd have to admit the thought of him with one of those blondes made her stomach twist in a very ugly way.

His nose nudged her earlobe. "Doesn't mean I don't find you attractive as well. That first day? I was ready to charm you right out of those jeans. Right up until Trent walked out of the back room and called your name. I realized who you were and squashed that feeling like a spider under my boot."

A shiver raked the length of her spine. She drew a shuddering breath as she attempted to shove all the unwanted emotions back down where they belonged. Neither could she resist the desire to learn more. About him. About his life. About who he was as a man. "Tell me about Ava."

He shifted again, setting his legs on either side of hers, then slid his arms around her waist and rested his chin on her shoulder. "She could be very sweet and giving. She always made me laugh. She's the reason I have Cammie, actually. She worked in a no-kill shelter. One day, she tells me about this little dog who'd been dumped by a family who grew tired of her once she stopped being a cute little puppy. Ava said she'd lay curled up in her kennel, wouldn't look at anybody or interact. A week later, Ava brought her home, said she couldn't stand to see the dog so sad."

Mandy couldn't resist a smile. "You fell in love. And you said it wasn't possible."

Marcus nodded to where Cammie lay snoozing contentedly at the edge of the blanket. "Tell me you could look at that face and take her back?"

She glanced at Cammie. Technically, she had a leash attached, but she hadn't left Marcus's side for a single second. "She really is a sweet little thing. She had no problem giving me a grand tour of the house."

He drew a deep breath and blew it out. "When Ava was manic, she tended to be very impulsive. She'd go on shopping sprees, buy things she didn't need. She stayed up late one night and bought all kinds of shit off those infomercials they play at two in the morning. She also loved to dance. She'd go to a club, drink until she could barely walk, then bring someone home with her. Some of the guys she ended up with were assholes."

His body tensed against her back. Mandy reached down to find his hand and curled her fingers around his. "I take it she lived with you at the time?"

"No. When I deployed, she stayed with Gram, but I heard about everything when I came home on leave. I ended up with Cammie because she up and decided one day I was hers." He let out a soft laugh, then sighed. His voice lowered to a pain-filled murmur. "When Ava was depressed, she wouldn't eat, to the point that she'd grow scary thin. Instead, she'd sleep all the time. When she was awake, she talked about suicide a lot. The doctors said it's hereditary. We think she got it from Mom, because Mom tended to act the same way."

"It wasn't your fault, you know, that she died."

"On some level, I know that, but I just can't convince myself of it. Gram was getting too old to have to deal with someone with the mentality of a child. She needed my help. It's why she lives so close."

He went eerily quiet, his heavy thoughts all but filling the air around him. Was he lost in the memories? She squeezed his fingers in support but waited him out.

"*Take care of your sister.* That's the last thing my mother said to me before she left that day. *She needs you. Take care of her.*"

The haunted, pain-filled words wrenched at her gut.

"My God, Marcus." Unable to hide her surprise and irritation, she twisted out of his embrace and turned, sitting sideways between his thighs. "That's a heavy burden to put on a child."

He made a sound of agreement from the back of his throat but didn't look at her. Instead, he sat staring at the lake.

She could only watch him for a moment, the pieces settling together like a jigsaw puzzle in her mind. It suddenly made sense why he'd closed himself off from the world. Why his relationship with Trent and the guys at the shop was so important and why he'd go through so much trouble for his grandmother. He'd essentially lost everybody he loved. The thought made her heart ache for him. When push came to shove, at least she had her family.

Unable to help herself, she turned to face him, setting her legs on either side of his hips. She laid her head on his chest, wound her arms around his ribs, and hugged him. "I won't tell him, you know. Trent, I mean. He's bound to find out. We all do too much together to be able to keep this a secret for long. But the news won't come from me."

His arms tightened around her. He ducked his head and pressed a kiss to her shoulder. "I appreciate that, but I'm pretty sure he knows already. I just haven't figured out what the hell to do about it."

She lifted her head to see his face. "I'm sorry. I wasn't thinking when I showed up this afternoon. I got carried away with the thought of surprising you."

She'd let herself get lost in the hunger between them. It was safer than the yearning. Than...this. The soul-wrenching honesty. The more she got to know Marcus, the more she liked him. Marcus was a good man.

He smiled again, this one wistful but amused, and stroked the shell of her ear with his index finger. "Are you always so impulsive?"

She let his amusement fuel her mood, hoping, somehow, to lighten the heaviness still hanging on him. More than that, though, she wanted to forget the need still pounding around in her chest. It was a desperate yearning that needed to be squashed before it became too big to ignore—to get to know more of him. "Yes. Life should be lived, grabbed by its ears and rode hard."

His body shook with his quiet laugh. "Only you could say something like that and not make it sound like a sexual innuendo."

She leaned in and nipped at his chin. "Who said it wasn't?"

His expression sobered. When he shifted his gaze to the lake again, Mandy's heart gave a painful thump. She'd expected him to toss out a provocative comeback or laugh. Instead, she got the feeling he was shutting her out again. It bothered her. Too much.

She stroked his cheek, his stubble course and prickly yet oddly soft beneath her palm. "Whatever you're thinking, I'd rather you say it. I understand you're not a talker, but I'm not fond of being shut out. Don't assume I won't want to hear whatever it is or that I won't understand. Friends talk to each other. I can handle anything you tell me so long as you're honest with me."

He blew out a heavy breath. His gaze flicked to her, something hard and challenging in the recesses she couldn't quite grasp. "I need you tonight. I'm also not fond of the term 'friend,' because it means I eventually have to watch you go back to dating those idiots again."

The words he hadn't spoken hung in the air between them, temptation itself. Mandy's heart hammered in her ears. God help her. She shouldn't ask. To do so would be pushing those boundaries again, but she had to hear him say the words. Just once. "Why does that bother you?"

Deep creases formed between his brows. The muscle in his jaw jumped, but he drew a deep breath and released it, the stiffness leaving his body. "Because some part of me says you're mine."

A heady shiver trailed her spine. That had to be sexiest thing any man had ever said to her. Nobody, save her high school sweetheart, Carter, had ever wanted her to be his. And even then, he'd eventually dumped her for a cheerleader. A response played in her mind, a dangerous answer for sure, but God help her, she had to say it.

She scooted closer, until her core rested against the front placket of his jeans and her mouth hovered over his. "Marcus?"

His gaze flicked to hers, then dropped. His hands slid down her back to settle over the curves of her ass. "Hmm?"

"For this month, I *am* yours." She brushed her mouth over his, whispering into the miniscule space between them. "So stop being such a damn gentleman and take me home. Make love to me or just take me to bed. I'm staying either way. Whatever you need, I'm good."

He studied her for the span of two pounding heartbeats. Just when she was sure he'd turn her down, he pressed a tender kiss to her lips. "Let's go."

She stood and held out her hand, pulling Marcus to his feet. He moved around her to scoop up a surprised-looking Cammie, tucking the dog in one arm, picking up the blanket with the other, then holding out his hand.

She stared for a beat before slipping her hand into his, and he started off for the parking lot. He'd taken her hand before, the night of the masquerade, when he'd pulled her out of Lauren's bakery, but this time felt different. Last time had been a demanding gesture. He'd forced her to follow him. This one was intimate. A connection.

He confirmed the thought when they reached his SUV. He released her hand long enough to open the rear door and set Cammie inside before turning to her again. Hunger warred with tenderness in his eyes as he cupped her face in his big hands and settled his mouth over hers. His tongue stroked her lower lip, and on a soft sigh, she sagged back against the car and opened for him.

His quiet groan rumbled through his chest, and his tongue thrust inside, bold and unapologetic. The kiss took flight from there. He devoured her, possessed her, and all she could do was hold on. Hands braced against his chest, she curled her fingers in an attempt to stay upright. She was sure her nails bit into his skin, but she couldn't think enough to make her fingers let go. Who was lost now?

When every bone in her body was limp and lifeless, he finally pulled back. Breathing hard, he dropped his forehead to hers and stood for a moment, staring at her. Mandy smoothed her hands up his back and smiled softly. "What was that for?"

"For being you." He brushed another kiss across her mouth, softer this time, then stepped back. "Come on. Let's go."

Five minutes later, as they headed toward his place, Marcus darted a glance at her and smiled, rueful and apologetic. "I ruined the plans you had for tonight. I'm sorry."

If that wasn't a big hint as to his mood, she didn't know what was. She braced an elbow on the console between the seats and pecked his cheek.

"You didn't ruin it. We can save it for another day, when you're more in the mood." Determined to keep his mind off his heavy thoughts, she winked at him. "Besides, it requires you to tell me your favorite fantasy."

He chuckled. "I'm surprised you haven't figured it out. I'm a simple man."

Oh, she had a pretty good idea. The moment in front of the mirror had given her a really big clue, but she wanted to hear him say the words.

Mandy grinned. "I'm guessing it involves watching."

"Something like that." A soft flush rose in his cheeks, but Marcus didn't look at her.

Mandy laughed quietly. "You aren't seriously embarrassed to admit that?"

"That's a very desperate thing to admit." He shot her a sideways glance, mouth pressed into a thin line, before turning back to the road. "Which is when I usually do it. When I'm desperate for relief from the thoughts you always manage to inspire."

Mandy squeezed his thigh. "That's not desperate. It's a turn-on." She leaned her mouth to his ear and lowered her voice. She'd bring this man out of his head if it killed her. "Tell me what it is. What do you think about while lying in the dark, hmm?"

She sat back in her seat again, and he darted another sidelong glance at her, brow still furrowed, eyes still too intense. What would it take to really break down his walls? It was a dangerous yearning, that one.

This time, though, he shook his head and muttered something under his breath about "pushing boundaries." Instead of answering her question, however, he picked up her hand from his leg and slid it to the apex of her thighs. "Does that tell you anything?"

A heady shiver ran the length of her spine. They really did have the same tastes. The suggestion had her imagination working overtime.

"As I suspected." Mandy stared at his profile, the idea percolating in the back of her mind. It had been rolling around in her thoughts since the first time they'd made love, in front of that mirror. She shouldn't follow it, but neither could she resist. Tonight, he wanted to get lost, and she would help him get there.

Decision made, she slid down in her seat, undid her pants, and pushed her hand into her panties. "You mean something like this?"

His gaze darted in her direction, eyes wide with panic. He groaned. "What are you doing?"

"We have the same fantasy. The thought of you, naked,

with that big, beautiful cock in your hand." She closed her eyes and strummed her clit as she immersed herself in the long familiar images. Her desire had gotten sidetracked but flooded her again now, and she let it. Desire, physical need, was better than the intimacy they'd created tonight. "That's not something to be ashamed of. That's fucking hot."

Somewhere outside, a car honked. Their car jerked and Marcus swore under his breath. "Jesus, Mandy, you're going to make me crash."

She ignored his comment and slid her fingers down her slit, pushing them inside herself. Pleasure erupted through her, and a quiet moan escaped. He set her body aflame, and her hunger for him burned through her blood. Knowing he watched now? That it aroused him as well? Her clit pulsed, throbbing with need. Every glide of her fingers sent pleasure and heat shivering over each nerve ending.

"God, do you know how wet that makes me? Tell me something. Do you immerse yourself in it the way I do? Take your time and enjoy every stroke?" She forced her eyes open and turned her head, staring at his profile. "Or are you forever the military man? Fast and efficient?"

He darted a glance over his shoulder and changed lanes. "A little of both."

A building caught her attention and Mandy turned her head to peer out the passenger side window. She passed that building on her way to work every morning. An abandoned industrial area. An idea she'd started with morphed.

She nodded in the direction of her window. "See that abandoned warehouse off to the right?"

"No."

She closed her eyes and pulled her fingers from her core, spread the slippery juices over her now swollen, throbbing clit and gasped. She had to admit the thought of unbuttoning Mr. Rules over there and getting to watch him come undone had her so hot she was panting. Her thighs trembled already. If he didn't pull off the highway soon, she'd come, and he probably would crash the car. "Just up there, on the right."

"I see it. That's the answer to what you're thinking." His voice came gruff and harsh, his words little more than a reprimand.

She opened her eyes and turned to stare at him. He sat glaring at the road, his jaw tight, shoulders tense. If she could get him to agree, she'd accomplish two things: help him out of his neat little box, and, if she were lucky, they'd forget about the growing intimacy between them. She softened her tone. "Do you trust me?"

He darted a glance at her. Stared for a beat. Then turned back to the road and blew out a heavy breath. The stiff set of his shoulders finally relaxed. "You know I do."

She slid her free hand over his knee. "Then trust me now. I want you, you want me, and I don't want to wait. We won't get caught if we're fast. I won't even take off my panties." She rolled her eyes. "Probably would have been easier if I'd worn a skirt, but you won't regret it. I promise."

He gripped the steering wheel so hard his knuckles turned white. Mandy held her breath, every inch of her caught somewhere between heady arousal and the gut-wrenching anticipation of his answer. It scared her how much she needed him to agree to this harebrained idea of hers. The whole notion had taken on another level. It had led her right back to the very thing she'd drummed up this idea to avoid—the growing intimacy between them.

Just when she thought he'd turn her down again, Marcus swore under his breath, flipped on his blinker, and jerked the wheel, moving onto the off-ramp. He darted another glance at her, his gaze intense but full of a tender heat. "You have about a minute to get those pants off."

She bit the inside of her cheek to keep from grinning and winked at him. Score one for her. "Yes, sir."

As she made quick work of her pants, Marcus exited the highway and turned right. The car bumped over a set of railroad tracks as he followed a long, dirt road to where the building sat against a wall of trees. The place sat on the edge of the city, two huge buildings that looked like they hadn't been used in years. The car's headlights illuminated the ground, the single streetlamp lighting the building and the parking lot in a soft glow. Grass and weeds had grown up in between the cracks in the pavement. The building itself was run-down, the metal siding coated with rust, more windows broken than intact.

Marcus drove around to the back and pulled the car into a spot at the far end of the lot, situating them between the building and the trees. Here they were no longer visible from the highway.

He shifted the car into park and looked over at her as he reached into his back pocket. His brow was still furrowed, his eyes still too intense, full of a heady mix of arousal and anxiety. "We'll need to be fast."

Mandy pulled her last leg from her pants, leaving them wadded on the floorboards, and laughed softly. "Trust me. This won't take long. You have me very aroused."

"Ditto, angel. What the hell brought this on, anyway?" He shook his head as he opened his pants, then lifted up enough to shove his jeans and underwear down his thighs. After rolling the condom onto his length, he pulled the mechanism to move the seat back as far as it would go, then held out a hand. "Come here."

Mandy's entire body trembled as she climbed over the center console. It wasn't an easy task, either. Her ass bumped the mirror, though luckily she managed to avoid the horn. By the time she straddled his thighs, her entire body buzzed with a heady rush of arousal and adrenaline. As she sat back on his knees, though, the truth hit her where it hurt. She would have to bare her heart and be honest with him now.

She rested her hands against the warmth of his chest, letting the solidity of him give her the courage to say the words. "You wanted to forget."

Marcus studied her, that intense, focused gaze working her face. "You're something else, you know that? Remind me to thank you properly when we get home." He captured her mouth, his kiss tender and sweet and soft. His big, warm hands settled on her ass, pulling her to him.

Needing him in a way that had her shaking all over again, Mandy reached down and moved her panties aside. Then she rose and slid onto him, taking him inch by delicious inch. She gasped at the sweet invasion, at the wondrous feeling of fullness. God, she'd never get tired of that feeling, of his thick cock deep inside of her. He filled every inch of her, rubbed tissues made extra sensitive by her overwhelming arousal.

Marcus groaned low in his throat and broke the kiss, setting his cheek hard against hers. "Christ you feel so fucking good."

Urgency moved between them like a living, breathing being. A slow, sweet rhythm. How the hell lovemaking could even be tender when they were essentially fucking in a car on the side of the road, she didn't know, but it was. His hands slid up her back, gathering her closer, until they sat chest to chest and nose to nose, and she took every breath with him. His gaze burned into hers as they rocked together.

With every slip of him inside of her, they clutched each other tighter. Her sensitized clit skimmed his pelvis, and a shower of hot sparks burst along her skin. Marcus groaned quietly, his breaths as harsh and ragged as her own, but not once did his gaze leave hers.

Every thrust seemed to propel them faster, until they strained against each other. The sounds of their combined breathing filled the car. The seat squeaked and the vehicle rocked. The windows fogged. It was the most erotic thing she'd ever done, because despite the darkness, he was with her the whole way.

Like a lit match tossed onto a dry field, her orgasm exploded through her. The most incredible, breath-stealing pleasure erupted along every sensitive nerve ending. Mandy bit her lip hard to keep from crying out as her inner muscles tightened and loosened, leaving her gasping and quaking in his arms.

Marcus groaned from down deep. His big hands gripped her ass hard. He held her there and cursed under his breath, his belly shaking as his own release claimed him.

He collapsed back against the seat, and Mandy dropped her forehead onto his shoulder. Several moments passed in fatigued silence, only their quiet panting filling the car's interior.

Just as her breathing returned to normal, Marcus began to laugh. It started as a chuckle, but very quickly became a deep, *this-side-of-delirious* kind of laugh that made his chest and shoulders shake.

Mandy sat back on his knees, unable to keep from grinning and giggling right along with him. She wasn't sure she'd ever seen Marcus come completely undone, but it stunned her all the same. Completely free, he was . . . magnificent. It lit up his whole face, relaxed him in a way she'd never seen before.

After several minutes, his laughter finally died. He drew a shuddering breath and blew it out, then pressed a tender, lingering kiss to her mouth. "I can't believe you made me do that."

Mandy furrowed her brow and shook her head slowly. "You really do need to learn to live a little."

"I bow to your experience, angel. Where you lead, I'll follow. Just promise you won't get me arrested, huh?" He kissed her softly again and smacked her ass. "Now get dressed. We need to get the hell out of here before the cops come. I don't know how the hell I'd explain *that* to Trent."

Mandy laughed and pecked Marcus's lips, then climbed carefully off his lap. As she slid into the passenger seat, she darted a glance at the backseat. Despite the goings-on in the front, Cammie lay curled up on a blanket, eyes closed.

Marcus pulled off the condom, knotted the end, and stuffed it in his pocket. As he did up his jeans, Mandy concentrated on shimmying into her skinny leather pants, but she didn't miss how silent Marcus had become again.

He pulled out of the parking spot, then made his way back to the quiet highway. Cammie made a yipping sound from the backseat, finally awake. Ears perking up, she set her front paws on the window's edge. Those big ears stood straight up, her brown eyes wide and round as she watched the scenery pass by.

Marcus reached over and took Mandy's hand. He glanced at her and smiled, so tender it melted another chunk of the wall she'd surrounded herself in a week ago. At some point, the way he got to her would be her downfall. She had a feeling she could easily fall in love with him if she let herself. Despite all the times he'd told her he was no good for her, Marcus was a decent man.

Because some part of me says you're mine.

Her heart warmed at his earlier words. She was pretty sure he was right. This simple moment, heading "home" with Marcus, filled her with a sense of belonging. This wasn't what they'd planned. Their relationship was supposed to revolve around hot, sweaty, glorious sex. And *only* sex.

Being with him this way, the soft intimacy, felt entirely too right. All those dreamy, girlish notions filled her thoughts all over again, simultaneously drawing and repelling her. She could see herself with him on a more permanent basis, and she hadn't a damn clue what to do about it.

CHAPTER ELEVEN

Mandy followed Marcus inside the house and toed off her shoes, leaving them beside the door. Marcus unclipped Cammie's leash and bent to scratch the dog's head. Neither of them had said anything during the twenty-minute ride home. For the first time in she didn't know how long, she hadn't a damn clue what to do with herself. She was comfortable in her own skin, comfortable with the opposite sex, but Marcus? He made her feel naked and exposed and way too vulnerable.

Marcus had that look. The one she'd seen too many times on Trent's face that first year after he'd gotten out of the service. The one that told her he was lost in the past. It made her heart ache. She didn't have to ask to know what—or who— he was thinking about.

She wanted to hug him, but she wasn't sure he wanted her to or that she should, so she kept her hands to herself. "You're quiet. Are you okay?"

Marcus finally straightened and turned to her. Small

creases formed between his brows, and the corners of his mouth turned down as he tucked his hands in his pockets. "I'm sorry. I got to thinking on the way here."

That he didn't touch her spoke volumes. Neither did he even attempt humor. All of which told her none too subtly he was putting back up that impossible wall. A wall that, the more she caught of it, the more she wanted to breach and finally move beyond. None of which she *should* want. This whole night was pushing boundaries she shouldn't allow, because in the end, she'd only get her heart broken.

Knowing all that didn't stop the wanting, though.

She drew a deep breath, tried to prepare herself for the disappointment, and stepped toward him. She fisted her hands to keep from reaching out and touching him. "Would you rather be alone?"

Seconds ticked out in unbearable silence. Those intense eyes searched hers. Finally, he blew out a defeated breath, shoulders rounding.

"No. I'd like you to stay, but..." He hooked her around the waist and tugged her close, settling his hands on the curves of her ass. "My head's not in a good place tonight."

She didn't have to ask to know what he needed. It was plain in the vulnerability in his eyes. He needed to hold and be held, to not have to sleep alone. She had the same need. It hit her more often these days.

Which was exactly why she *ought* to be going home.

God, did she really want to travel this road with him? Once she set this in motion, there was no going back. Another glance at the pain hanging all over him sealed the deal. She couldn't *not* do this.

"Tell me what you need, Marcus." She had a feeling she knew, but she needed to hear him say the words.

"You."

She rolled her eyes, but couldn't stop her half smile all the same. "How?"

He studied her for so long she was sure he'd shut her out, make some excuse. Finally, he sighed. His gaze locked on hers, those eyes intense and focused.

"I want to bury myself so damn deep inside of you I lose all track of myself. I want to feel you wrap your body around me, and I want to make you come so hard you scream my name. Because what I really want . . . is to get lost. Until I can't think any more about the shit parading through my head. But I'm entirely too aware how selfish it is to want that, and I'm too damn tired for any of it." He huffed a laugh and cocked a brow. "Sorry you asked?"

"Not even a little bit. You hold too much in." She smiled, lifted onto her toes, and pressed a kiss to his lips, then stepped back and held out a hand. "How 'bout we just go to bed, hmm?" Marcus slid his hand into hers and Mandy glanced down at Cammie, who had yet to leave their sides. "You too. Bedtime."

Mandy turned and made her way toward the bedroom. Cammie followed close on her heels. Once inside, Cammie leapt onto the bed, headed straight for the pillows, and plopped down. Mandy smiled before turning to Marcus. He didn't argue when she reached for the waistband of his jeans or even attempt to stop her when she helped him out of them. He simply stood, watching her with those tired eyes. She took a moment to take off her own pants, crossed to the door, and flicked off the light, then grabbed his hand and pulled him to the bed.

She slid beneath the covers, waiting as Marcus crawled in beside her. He lifted his arm, and she settled against his side, resting her head in the crook of his shoulder.

After a moment, he drew a breath and released it. "It almost feels wrong to be here with you this way. A friend is dead. His wife is lying alone in her bed tonight, probably wondering how the hell she's going to make it without him, and here I am with you. Living my life. Enjoying it."

Mandy settled a hand against his chest, fingers stroking back and forth. "Guilt. That's normal, you know."

He cupped her face in the warmth of his palm, his thumb caressing along her jawline and skimming her bottom lip. "Mmm. So they told me after Ava died. Not that it stops me from feeling it. I can't help wondering if we missed something. If there's something we could've done to stop him. If he'd just... reached out. Called someone. Any one of us would've been there in a heartbeat."

She stroked her hand up his belly to his chest. "It's not your fault, and you shouldn't blame yourself. I've watched you with the guys from the shop for a while now, and I can tell you're a good friend. The choice was ultimately his. For whatever reason, he felt that was his only way out."

He let out a harsh laugh. "Yeah, they told me that, too, when Ava died. How'd you get so smart, anyway?"

Mandy shrugged. "When Trent came home, I worried about him, so I did some research, spoke with a therapist who gave me some tips, things to look for, et cetera. In the end, though, it was his choice, whether or not he wanted to live. I just tried my damnedest to make sure he knew there were people who cared."

He sighed. "Exactly what bugs the shit out of me. I didn't, and I shouldn't have missed the signs, because Ava had them, too."

She turned her head, pressing a kiss to his chest. "It wasn't your fault."

"I know, but I've lost too damn many people." He lay silent, staring at the ceiling, before he turned his head toward her. "Which is why I'm not willing to risk losing your friendship."

The gruff, no-nonsense tone of his voice made her chest ache. He was reaffirming his "rules," had set her back in her place and reminded her of the painful end, coming up fast. Eventually, she had to let him go, and the thought made her hurt all over. The sad truth stared her in the face, and she couldn't deny it anymore. She didn't want only his friendship. She wanted him. All of him.

Trying desperately to ignore the tangle of emotion coiling through her belly, she slid over the top of him, lying along his length, and stroked his bottom lip with a finger. "I refuse to argue with you. You're worrying for nothing on that front. I'm not planning on going anywhere. Believe me, I've got the friendship thing down pat."

Instead of answering, Marcus slid a hand to the back of her

neck and pulled her to him, capturing her mouth. Deep and demanding and encompassing, his kiss stole her breath. His lips tangled with hers in an erotic play that made her forget to breathe. He sipped slowly, his supple mouth sliding over hers. Flicked his tongue against her bottom lip. Nibbled at one corner. Only to move back to those tender sips and tastes.

Mandy sighed into the connection and melted into him. By the time he finally came up for air again, she'd lost all sense of herself. There was only him. Breathless and shivering with an ultra-heightened sense of vulnerability, she dropped her forehead to his. "What was that for?"

His big, warm hands caressed her back, that intense, probing gaze burning through her for a moment. "I needed you today."

"Anytime." She pressed a soft, lingering kiss to his lips, then slid to his side again and laid her head on his shoulder. "I mean that."

He was silent a moment. "Will you be here after the funeral?"

The bare whisper of his voice told her in no uncertain terms how hard it was for him to even ask.

She slid her hand over his belly and squeezed him tight. "I'll be here."

Marcus wrapped both arms around her and pressed a kiss into her hair. "Thank you. I'm not sure I could do it alone this time."

* * *

Marcus halted in the kitchen entrance. The sight on the opposite end of the room calmed the choking haze of panic he'd woken with. Mandy stood at the stove with her back to him, wearing nothing but a midriff T-shirt and a pair of sexy, lacy panties. This morning's pair allowed him a peek of her shapely ass. The scent of eggs and butter permeated the space, the sound of sizzling filling the silence as Mandy bebopped to a tune only she could hear.

He folded his arms and leaned against the doorway to watch her for a moment. He'd dreamed last night, something he hadn't done in months. His PTSD came and went with no consistency. He'd have months of nightmares, of being hyper-aware of the world around him, when every little noise was a grenade going off beside him. And then he'd have months of being perfectly fine.

Lately, he'd had a reprieve, but Jason's suicide had brought it all back. This time, though, it was Ava he'd seen in his dreams. Her face had hovered over him last night, as if she stood beside the bed, smiling and happy. Right before the dream morphed into his worst nightmare.

It relieved the panic more than a little to find Mandy in his kitchen. She looked damn domestic, too, barefoot and half naked, curls mussed, cooking breakfast.

She looked entirely too right there.

He crossed the room, slid his arms around her waist, and buried his nose in her hair. His lungs filled with the scent of her, and the panic caging his chest eased.

Mandy jumped, darting a glance behind her, then blew out a breath and swatted his arm. "You scared the hell out of me."

He rested his chin on the top of her head but couldn't bring himself to release her entirely. "Sorry. Just needed to touch you."

She turned her head, her forehead resting against his chin. "You were restless last night. Are you okay?"

"Mm." He skimmed his nose down her neck, immersing himself in the heady scent of her skin, its incredible softness. She deserved honest answers, not his diversion tactics, but it still wasn't easy to lay his emotions out before someone. Especially her. Mandy had wormed her way inside. Her body beside him in bed at night felt too good, like she belonged there, and her opinion mattered. If she thought him weak, he didn't want to see the echo of it in her eyes.

All of which meant she'd become important and none of which he knew what the hell to do with. "I dreamed last night."

She took a moment to turn off the burner and slid the skillet aside, then laid her arms over his where they rested at her waist. "What about?"

He followed her jawline to her ear, down the length of her neck to the curve in her shoulder. That soft vanilla and something uniquely her filled his nostrils with every breath and the last of the tension in his chest left him. "Ava. They come and go. It's always the same one."

Some part of his brain warned him, again, that he shouldn't share, that he ought to keep their relationship simple. But there was something about her. The trouble she'd gone through for him yesterday flat-out awed him, and the lure of her pulled the words from his mouth anyway.

He sighed and straightened, pulled her back against him and rested his chin on the top of her head. "She's always lost. I can hear her calling to me from somewhere far off, pleading for help, but I can never find her. In the end, I never get to her in time."

"You'll see her again. Happy and whole." Her fingers stroked the skin of his forearms, lightly caressing the hairs there. Gentle. Soothing. Enough to send shivers up his arms. "That's what Mom told us when Grandma died. That we'd see her again. Made me feel better when I was little, at least."

"Heaven." He nodded, his mind filling with memories. "When we were little, Gram made Ava and me go to church with her. Said it was important that we learn, so that we can decide for ourselves someday. She used to tell us something similar, that there was a place we all went when we died."

"But you don't believe."

"I don't know what to believe." He didn't think God, if there was one, wanted someone like him. He was pretty sure he'd failed several parts of that particular bargain. He'd killed people. Wasn't that one of the Ten Commandments? Did it matter that they'd fired the first shots? Or that he'd done it to protect innocents? "It's a nice thought, though, that Ava's whole and happy somewhere. Not in pain anymore."

"Speaking of your grandmother." Mandy pulled away enough to turn in his arms, settled her palms against his chest, and smiled up at him, eyes alight. "When do I get to meet her, anyway?"

Yeah, okay, so he'd been putting the meeting off. The thought of taking this charade into reality made him more than a little nervous. When he'd made that date with Military Match, he'd wanted Gram off his case. Now? Hell. The thought of actually lying to her—something he promised her a long time ago he'd never do—no longer sat well with him. He still wanted Gram to relax, to not worry about him so much, but the truth was, his relationship with Mandy didn't feel so phony anymore.

It was a fine line he was walking. For the first time in a long time, Mandy had him pondering his future and what he wanted from it. Was spending his life alone still what he wanted? When this month ended, would he really be able to let her go? To pretend she meant nothing to him more than a good roll in the sack?

That was the trouble. He didn't know anymore.

He tucked a wayward curl behind her ear. "Gram said to bring you over for Sunday dinner. If that's good for you?"

Mandy nodded. "Sunday's great. I have a wedding on Saturday, and Friday will likely be the last-minute cram to make sure everything goes smoothly."

He cupped her face in his hands, stroked his thumbs over her cheeks, for a moment lost in the incredible softness, in the light in her eyes. Then he pressed a gentle kiss to her lips. He was grateful to her. For so many damn reasons. "Thank you."

"For what?"

"This. And last night. I needed you, and you didn't hesitate." He'd grown up determined to rely only on himself. After all, Gram had had Ava to take care of; he hadn't wanted to be another burden. Now here was Mandy, pushing past all his defenses in an effort to save him from himself. She awed him.

Mandy smiled, this one soft and understanding, and stroked her thumbs across his chest. "I told you. Anytime."

"So you did." He stared at her for a long moment, studying the lines and angles of her face. The emotion beat behind his breastbone like the pulse of his heart, steady, just beneath the surface. It had been beating around in his brain all night.

Mandy had ended up in his dreams as well. She'd hovered beyond his peripherals, a presence he could hear but not see. Calm and soothing, like an angel of mercy. He wasn't sure he wanted to face the emotions he'd woken with. The panic at not finding her beside him. The desperate need to go in search of her.

He shouldn't give them voice, either, but he couldn't deny he felt them anymore. She made him want. Her sweet smile and soft kisses. The comfort of her beside him. And he wanted it every night.

He wanted her to be his, to claim her.

Despite the voice in the back of his mind screaming at him not to say the words, he dropped his forehead to hers and gave in to the pull to share. "I won't deny you make me feel something, angel, that part of me wants...more. But I've done this before, and all I did was end up hurting her. I vowed to myself I'd never do it again, make promises I couldn't keep. The last thing I want to do is hurt you like that, or risk losing your friendship when we figure out I'm just not relationship material."

Mandy stared for a beat, those eyes reaching and searching, in that way of hers that made him feel naked. Like she could see all those vulnerable places inside. What scared the hell out of him was how intensely he wanted to let her see, to let her in. She was the first woman in more than four years to make it past his defenses, and God help him, but he liked her there.

She dropped her gaze and smoothed her fingers across his chest. "This isn't ideal. I'll give you that. But I enjoy this for what it is. I enjoy *you*. I'm not sorry I got involved with you. Not even a little bit. The fantastic sex is the icing on the cake." She winked at him, sassy and full of herself. "So stop worrying about it and let yourself enjoy this."

She patted his chest, her gaze a wash of emotion. Tenderness. Honesty. Even a hint of that playful impishness he adored. Then she rose onto her toes and pressed her mouth to his, a soft, lingering peck, released him, and turned back to the stove.

As she reached for the skillet she'd set aside, she darted a glance over her shoulder. "You pour the coffee. I'll dish out the eggs."

CHAPTER TWELVE

Marcus's heart jackhammered his rib cage as he pulled into the driveway behind Mandy's candy-apple-red Toyota. The sight of it made his cock swell behind his zipper as need expanded, burning through his blood. It was only Friday. He'd anticipated another two days before he got to see her again. He'd been trying not to, but he couldn't deny he'd missed her. Without her, his world went back to being cold and empty. He'd come to that stark realization while lying in the dark staring at his damn ceiling.

A part of him had died with Ava that day four years ago. Mandy was a bright spot in his world, a blip of sun. Beautiful. Enchanting. She made him want to actually live, instead of simply existing. He was going to allow himself to enjoy the time he had with her, but he wouldn't—couldn't—risk losing her friendship.

And he would if he allowed his feelings for her to grow any further. Because it never failed. He always managed to fuck relationships up. He'd failed Ava.

He exited the car and opened the rear passenger door, scooping Cammie off her blanket in the backseat. "Come on, girl. Looks like we've got company."

She wagged her little tail and he set her on the ground, then locked the car and jogged up the front walk. He called out as he entered the foyer, "Mandy?"

When she didn't answer, he started for the kitchen, but something out of place in the living room caught his eye, halting him dead in his tracks. Some twenty feet or so across the space, Mandy sat in the recliner.

In nothing but the blue silk tie he'd worn to the masquerade and a sultry smile.

With one leg bent up against her belly and the other dangling over the edge of the chair, he had a fantastic view of the lovely heart she'd carved on her mound. His mouth watered and his heavy thoughts flitted away as quickly as they'd come.

She fingered the end of the tie. "Evening, Marcus."

Cammie took one look at her, spun in an excited circle, and ran, leaping onto the chair and straight into Mandy's lap. She set her feet on Mandy's very bare belly and leaned up to lick her chin, her tail wagging.

Marcus chuckled as he closed the front door and moved into the front room. "Look at you. What on earth are you doing here?"

Mandy's smile faltered as she attempted to greet Cammie while dodging the dog's kiss attack. "I wanted to see you."

He stopped in front of the chair and pointed at the floor. "Cam, down."

If dogs could pout, he was pretty sure Cammie gave him

one as she reluctantly hopped from the recliner and sat with a little huff at his feet. He leaned one hand on the chair's arm and bent over Mandy. The desperate need to be as close as humanly possible fired through him, but he forced himself to move slowly, lest he scare them both. "I'm sorry about her. She's not very well mannered."

Mandy stared, wide-eyed, her chest rising and falling at a rapid pace. "I'm sorry. I wanted to surprise you, but I kind of forgot about her."

"What happened to Sunday?" He bent closer, hovering now over the soft temptation of her mouth and, unable to resist, trailed his fingers over her bare curves. Over her soft shoulder, down her bare belly, and between her thighs. He plunged two fingers inside her heat and groaned. God, she was wet.

She gasped, her hips bowing into his hand. "I c-couldn't wait."

"Well, I'm glad." Unable to hold back any longer, he brushed his mouth over hers once, twice. "I've been dying to see you."

She angled her chin, reaching for him, her voice now a breathless whisper. "Missed me, did you?"

Missed wasn't quite the way he'd put it. He craved her beyond something that made sense. He wanted the connection, when he sank into her and her body rose to his and something more powerful than gravity pulled them together. It wasn't like that with any other woman, and he yearned to see the reflection of it in her eyes.

"You tell me." He took her hand and guided it to the bulge

in his pants. "That sprang up the minute I saw your car in the driveway."

She cupped his erection, massaging and stroking him through his jeans. "Have you...?"

"No. I'd much rather..." Marcus released a shaky breath and dropped his forehead to her shoulder as his whole body focused on that one fine point. Her hand on his cock for what felt like the first time in ages. "Shit."

She leaned her mouth to his ear, her breath a hot, erratic huff against his neck, and kept stroking. "You'd rather what?"

"Have you." One stroke of her hand, one look at the heady mix of desire and vulnerability in her eyes, and she had him right where she no doubt wanted him. Completely at her mercy.

Her warm mouth covered his earlobe, teeth gently scraping the sensitive flesh. Her hand released him, only to reach for the button on his jeans. One rough tug and she had his fly open. Seconds later, her warm, supple fingers slid around his engorged cock, setting off a shower of hot sparks from the point of contact outward. She stroked him slowly, her fingers gliding over super-sensitive skin. "Let it go, Marcus. I need this. I need *you*."

He swore under his breath. He'd wanted to take this slow, to enjoy every supple inch of her, but like that night at Gabe's barbeque, he didn't have the strength to resist. He pumped into her hand, thrusting in time with the stroke of her fingers.

It didn't take long. Her luscious soft skin conspired against him. His orgasm exploded over him, leaving him shaking and gasping and emptying himself into the warmth of her hand.

When the spasms ended, his legs dropped out from beneath him and Marcus landed on his knees. He laid his head in her lap as he attempted to catch his breath. All the while, she sifted the fingers of her free hand through his hair, her long nails gliding along his scalp, the sensation soothing and tender.

When he found the strength to move again, he kissed her thigh and smiled up at her. "How is it you always seem to bring me to my knees, angel?"

Amusement glinted in her eyes as her hand caressed his face, along the back of his ear to his neck. "Just good, I guess."

"Come on." After pushing to his feet, he leaned over her and captured her mouth for a lingering kiss, then straightened and held out his hand. "Let's go clean you up. Then you're next."

He pulled her to her feet and led her into the master bathroom. As she moved to the sink to wash her hands, he sidled up behind her. He bent his head, skimming his mouth along the side of her neck. Nipped at her deliciously bare shoulder. Cupped her full ass in his hands and massaged the muscle before sliding his hands up her flat stomach to her breasts.

When his palms grazed her hardened nipples, she moaned softly and leaned back into him, reached behind her, and slid her hand around the nape of his neck. Her image in the mirror drew him. Her back arched, pushing her breasts into his palms. Her warm, satiny skin on display. Her generous ass nestled against his pelvis.

"You're gorgeous, you know that?" He nudged her earlobe

with his nose before nibbling his way down her neck and across her shoulder. "All this glorious skin. So damn soft. I'd fuck you right here in front this mirror just so I could watch your face when you came, if I didn't want to taste you so badly."

She moaned again, this one soft and throaty, and pushed her ass back into him. He slid his hands down her belly to her hips and pulled her hard against him. Already his cock swelled behind his zipper again, as if reaching for her.

"Come on, angel. I'm suddenly starving." He winked at her reflection, then gripped her by the shoulders to hold her steady as he stepped back. When she straightened and faced him, he took her hand and led her into the bedroom. There he pulled her close, allowed himself a taste of her mouth, then nodded at the bed. "Lie down."

"Yes, sir." Playful impishness glinted in her eyes as she rose onto her tiptoes and flicked her tongue against his bottom lip. Then she turned, crawled up onto the bed on her hands and knees, and lay back. With her head tipped so that her gaze caught his, she bent her knees and dropped them open, reached down and stroked a finger along her slit.

A low growl escaped him. A fucking growl. He wanted to laugh. His need for her had made him a goddamn beast, but holy Christ she was gorgeous. Supple thighs spread, fingers stroking soft and slow. Her intimate folds glistened in the low light drifting in from the attached bathroom, and his mouth watered.

"Tease." He crawled up onto the bed and nipped at the flesh of her right thigh before settling himself on his stomach. He moved her hand out of the way and dipped his tongue in for a taste. Her flavor exploded on his tongue. Musky. Sweet. A quiet groan escaped him. "God, I can't believe how many times I've made love to you, and I've never taken the time to taste you."

She gasped, one hand sliding into his hair. "Would this be your favorite fantasy, then?"

He darted a glance at her. She lay with her eyes squeezed shut, thighs dropped open in abandon. She was fucking beautiful.

"No." He dipped his tongue in again, this one a long, slow stroke from the bottom up. He pushed his tongue inside, gathering her juices, and ended with a light flick over her swollen clit.

This earned him a quiet moan. Her fingers curled into his scalp. "Now who's the tease?"

He couldn't resist a grin. "Clearly if you can still talk I'm not doing my job properly."

He leaned in again, this time pushing his tongue deep, savored the flavor of her for a moment, before circling her sweet, tight little bud with light, teasing strokes. He wanted her writhing, wanted to draw out her pleasure, so that when her orgasm finally overcame her, it was over the top. He wanted her breathless and gasping.

Mandy panted, her fingers clutching the hair on the top of his head, holding him to her. He finally drew her clit into his mouth and sucked hard, then let her pop free. "Jesus, angel. You taste sweeter than my grandmother's apple pie."

She let out a strangled gasp. Her hips arched into his mouth. "Don't tease. Please."

With his right hand, he stroked her inner thigh. "Do you trust me?"

She moaned, this one tormented and needy and frustrated. "Yes, but—"

"No buts. Just trust me." He pushed a finger deep into her, stroked her inner walls, and fluttered his tongue over and around, again and again. The desperate little gasp she let out made him want to beat his damn chest. Her thighs began to shake, along with her belly.

Another flick of his tongue and a needy moan slid out of her. That sound was his undoing. Shaking right along with her, he slid one hand beneath her ass, lifting and angling her, and gave in to the hunger burning through him. He buried his mouth in her heat, licking and sucking with abandon. It would probably scare the hell out of him at some point, but he needed her pleasure almost more than she did.

A second hand joined the first, gripping his head. Her legs slid out straight, her knees locking, and those sweet, addicting sounds became low, throaty moans. Mandy went as rigid and still as a statue and, with another flick of his tongue and a stroke of her inner walls, began to shake.

"Marcus..." She moaned his name over and over as she gasped and sighed and shook.

It was fucking glorious. He yearned to be able to watch the pleasure travel across her face, but concentrated on her, stroking her through every luscious pulse, desperate to draw it out as long as possible.

With a sharp, indrawn breath, she finally went limp and closed her legs, pushing him back. Every bit as breathless as she was, he moved up the bed and dropped beside her, gathered her to him and wrapped his arms tightly around her.

"Oh my God." She draped her arm over his belly, slid her thigh over his, and let out a breathless laugh. "You really want to know what I like so much about older men?"

He kissed the top of her head. Truth was, he had no desire to know or to have the thought of her with other men parading through his mind. To be polite, though, he had to ask. "What's that, angel?"

"That." She giggled again, the sound glorious in its girlishness. "Sooo that."

Some part of him understood she'd meant her comment as a compliment, but his chest constricted all the same. The thought of her with anybody else made him want to hit something. Namely the next asshole to lay his hands on her. Their arrangement meant eventually she'd go back to dating other men. Spending her nights in their beds. Making love to someone else. Laughing at his jokes. Hell, eventually, she'd find someone she wanted to marry.

And he'd have to let her. Because he wasn't any good for her.

He glared at the ceiling, libido thoroughly doused. "I take it most of the idiots you date don't."

She lifted her head, frowning up at him. "Why do you insist on calling them idiots?"

He tilted his head to meet her gaze. "Because any man who takes his pleasure at the expense of his partner is."

She leaned up on an elbow, her gaze following the movements of her fingers as she caressed the side of his face and over his chin. Her voice became a husky whisper between them. "You're the only one, you know. Who's ever admitted I had that effect on him, when you said I bring you to your knees, I mean. I haven't had that in a while, a man who allowed himself to be vulnerable with me."

It would seem he didn't have a choice where she was concerned.

Long moments passed in silence, somewhere between comfortable companionship and a sweet, aching tension. The kind of tension filled with everything they weren't telling each other. Because they weren't supposed to. Because this was just supposed to be about sex.

Mandy dropped her gaze, effectively breaking the tense moment, and sifted her fingers through the hair on his chest.

"It's why I came over. I missed you, missed that feeling. I probably shouldn't tell you that, considering our arrangement, but if you really want to know why I'm here, that's it." She frowned and shook her head slowly. "It's been a hell of a week. I had a bridezilla to tame. Her wedding's tomorrow, and the only part of it I'm looking forward to is when it's over. I just wanted to see you before I had to deal with it."

The soft honesty in her tone set his heart hammering. He'd looked forward to her, too. For very similar reasons. Nothing about the engine he and the guys at the shop were rebuilding had gone the way it should have. It had been an uphill battle the whole way, with a very impatient customer who kept calling to ask when it would be completed.

He'd been looking forward to this exact moment. When he'd have Mandy in his arms. When he could get lost in...every damn thing about her. The feel of her body against him. Her soft mouth. The ring of her laughter.

All of which meant he was already in way over his head. She'd become...too important. He'd have to put a stop to this sooner or later, but he didn't have the strength to do it now. Maybe it was selfish, but he wanted the rest of the month with her. Then he'd let her go, as planned. Because that's what he wanted...wasn't it?

CHAPTER THIRTEEN

Mandy drew a deep breath and blew it out as she climbed from the car. She halted at the end of the front walk, eyeing the house before her. Marcus's grandmother's house. Not surprisingly, given the things Marcus had told her, the place had a warmth to it. Coffee colored with white trim and lush green plants hanging from baskets in the fascia. On either side of the door sat two tall, round ceramic pots containing fat, brightly colored flowers. On the other half of the three-by-five porch was a padded chair and a small end table holding another plant with a single, white bloom.

The neighborhood reminded her a lot of the one her parents lived in. One of the few where the houses didn't all look the same. Children's laughter rang through the cool evening air from somewhere close, telling her the neighborhood was likely filled with families. Across the street, a large German shepherd pulled a woman down the sidewalk, his nose to the ground.

Having gotten Cammie out of the backseat, Marcus came

to a stop beside her. Cammie trotted past them, climbing the porch, and pawed at the door.

Both of them looked a lot calmer than she felt.

Her every limb seemed to be shaking, and her heart hammered from the vicinity of her tonsils. Two weeks ago, when she'd agreed to do this, it had seemed so simple. How hard could it be to pretend to be his girlfriend? She'd had a crush on him anyway, so it hadn't seemed like it would be a huge stretch to pretend to be enamored with him.

Now? Well, now her feelings for Marcus had changed, and their relationship didn't feel so phony anymore. His grandmother's first impression of her suddenly meant everything.

As if he sensed her gaze, Marcus looked over at her. "You ready for this?"

"Piece of cake." She let out a laugh that sounded half panicked even to her and glanced down at herself, toying with the hem of the silk camisole she'd donned an hour ago. "Do I look okay? I tried to pick something conservative. I've haven't done the whole *meet the parents* thing since high school."

She'd chosen a top like the one she'd worn to Gabe's barbeque, because she'd caught the look in Marcus's eyes that night. The undisguised hunger there had made her feel beautiful. She'd wanted to hold on to that tonight. She'd topped the camisole with a blazer and a black pencil skirt, but was the outfit "meet the family" material?

Marcus's eyes glinted with amusement, crinkling at the corners. He stared a beat before pressing a soft kiss to her lips.

"You look beautiful." His gaze flicked down her body. "Are you wearing a bra under that?"

"Yes." Mandy pulled her shoulders back. Of course she was. That was a girl thing. Girls could always tell when you weren't and tended to judge each other harshly for it. Among her closest friends she could go braless, because nobody cared, but Marcus's grandmother might. He'd said she was old-fashioned, and back in the day they trussed themselves up like chickens. Didn't they?

He faced the house again, but one corner of his mouth hitched. "Damn."

Mandy couldn't help her smile. Whether he'd done it on purpose or not, his teasing lightened her mood and her nerves flitted away on the breeze. Instead, that night at Gabe's bar-beque invaded her thoughts. His hand pushing beneath her shirt. The unbelievable pleasure when his warm palm curved around her breast for the first time.

She bumped his shoulder. "Tease."

He bumped her back, then tossed her a crooked grin. "Relax. It's just my grandmother."

Mandy eyed the house again. "What if she doesn't like me?"

Several seconds of silence ticked out, filling with a thick, palpable tension. She shouldn't have asked him that. It told him in no uncertain terms that this meeting meant something to her, far more than it should, and they'd already told each other too much lately.

Cammie whined and pawed at the door again.

Marcus looked over at her, stared for a beat, then turned to Mandy. He cupped her face in his big, warm hands and settled his mouth over hers. His kiss was slow and tender, a tangle of lips that had her sighing and melting into him. Until there was nothing left *but* him and the warm press of his mouth.

When he finally pulled back, her knees wobbled. Hands caught between them, she let out a breathless laugh. "That helped the panic, but I'm afraid it created another teensy problem."

Still so close his breath teased her lips, Marcus chuckled. "Good. Now, relax. Trust me. She'll love you."

He pecked her lips again, straightened, and slipped his hand into hers, tugging her behind him as he climbed the front porch steps. Stopping before the door, he knocked three times, then pushed the door open and poked his head inside. "Gram?"

"In the kitchen, sweetheart," a soft feminine voice called from the back of the house. "Did you bring your girl with you?"

He shook his head as he stepped into the foyer. "Yeah, Gram. I brought Mandy with me."

Cammie, who'd been waiting patiently up until that point, pushed past them and scampered inside.

An older woman popped her head around a wall, some twenty feet or so across from the foyer they stood in. Neatly carved gray brows raised as she bent to scratch Cammie's head. "Mandy...short for Amanda?"

His grandmother was pretty, from what little Mandy could see of her. The woman had the same sky-blue eyes Marcus had, but her hair won the bid for Mandy's attention. Marcus's eighty-year-old grandmother had a short pixie cut, the top gelled into spikes. Eccentric indeed.

Mandy squeezed Marcus's fingers tight to stem the nervous trembling moving through her body and aimed for a friendly smile. "Nope. Just Mandy. It's nice to finally meet you."

"Oh, honey. You have no idea how good it is to meet you." As she straightened, Gram smiled so wide it nearly split her face in half. She finally stepped out of the kitchen, drying her hands on a brightly colored hand towel.

Given everything he'd told her, Mandy expected his grandmother to be a frail old woman who used a cane and hobbled when she walked. As she closed the distance between them, though, his grandmother moved with the sure gait of a woman twenty years younger. She came to a stop in front of Mandy, took a moment to tuck the towel into the pocket of a pink apron covered in cupcake drawings, then enveloped Mandy in a surprisingly firm hug.

"This is a day I thought for sure would never arrive." Gram leaned back, holding Mandy by the shoulders. Her gaze filled with so much warmth the same emotion flooded Mandy's chest. "He hasn't brought someone home in eons. I've been worried about this boy."

Beside her, Marcus let out a miserable groan. "TMI, Gram, and I'm forty. I passed *boy* a long time ago."

Gram pursed her lips and tossed Marcus a look Mandy had seen one too many times on her mother's face. It said clearly, *Don't argue with me.* "You may not like it, son, but you will always be that little boy who came to live with me thirty years ago. I don't care how old or how big you get."

Marcus heaved a sigh and looked over at Mandy. "Forty years old, and she still manages to make me feel like I'm ten."

The warm familiarity of the exchange had a giggle popping out of Mandy, to which Marcus shot her a playful glare. Mandy covered her mouth but couldn't stop another giggle. "Sorry, but she's right. My mother still calls me her baby, and Dad still calls me 'sport.'"

Marcus frowned, amusement glinting in his eyes. "You're supposed to be on my side."

Gram rolled her eyes and shifted her gaze to Mandy. "How did you two meet? I'm afraid he hasn't told me a thing about you."

Gram's innocent question had guilt tightening in her stomach. She'd signed up for this, had promised to play this part, but damn it all to hell, she liked this woman. The thought of lying to Gram had nausea swirling in her stomach. She was going to hell for sure.

She smiled to cover her unease. "Well, we were fixed up through a dating service. Military Match? But we've actually known each for a while. My brother works at the repair shop."

"She's Trent's little sister," Marcus added beside her.

"Trent. Really? And then you met again through the dating site. Interesting." Gram shifted her gaze to Marcus, one brow arched. "If that isn't fate giving you a shove."

Mandy pressed her lips together to stifle another giggle. Now she knew where Marcus got *that* look from.

Glancing at Marcus, she found him frowning in disapproval. That pink flush had crept into his cheeks again. He opened his mouth, but before he could say anything, Gram's gaze shifted to Mandy. "What is it you do, dear?"

"Oh, I'm a wedding planner." This, at least, was an easy question.

The pleased gleam that illuminated Gram's eyes would have put the sun to shame. She turned her head again and pinned Marcus with a direct stare. The corners of her mouth twitched, but to her credit, she didn't smile. "Wedding planning. You don't say."

Marcus rolled his eyes. "Oh, here we go. Tell her how many great-grandkids you want, Gram."

Gram's lips twitched again, but she waved a flippant hand in the air. "Well, of course I want a dozen, but I'll settle for two."

"And we have to name one of them after my sister." Marcus nudged Mandy with an elbow and looked over at her, a teasing gleam in his eyes.

Both watched her in expectation of an answer, both gazes lively and amused. An emotion Mandy couldn't share. While some part of her understood they were only teasing, the images their words inspired invaded her thoughts. A five-year-old girl with Marcus's unusual blue-brown eyes and Mandy's dark curls. Marcus would hoist the girl high up over his head. Her delighted giggles rang through Mandy's mind.

The trembling started in her hands, slowly spreading outward to seemingly every part of her. It terrified her how badly she wanted that. With him.

The knowledge had her mind spinning in a million different directions. This went beyond merely wanting more with him than a casual fling. This was the whole enchilada.

Marcus's brow furrowed with concern. "You okay?"

Looking into those eyes, she knew. She'd gone and done the one thing she swore she wouldn't. She'd fallen in love with him.

That evening in Gabe's bathroom, when they'd made this agreement in the first place, flitted through her thoughts. His words filled her mind. *"That won't ever be me, angel."*

The thought of never again getting to experience moments like this—with him *and* his wonderful grandmother—made her chest ache.

Gram pursed her lips and gripped Mandy's hand, breaking her out of her tangled thoughts. "Now I've gone and made you uncomfortable. I'm sorry, sweetheart. It's a playful argument between Marcus and me. He's been determined to stay single for so long I can't help teasing him."

Mandy smiled, praying it looked remotely friendly and not as terrified as she felt. "It's okay. It's just..."

She looked over at Marcus, whose expression had gone carefully blank. She'd seen that look enough times now to recognize it. He was good at schooling his emotions. The SEAL in action no doubt, but seeing it filled her with that impossible need all over again. To be let in. To have all of him.

She turned back to Gram and offered an apologetic shrug. "We haven't exactly gotten that far. He just talks about you so much, I wanted to meet you."

Gram released her hand, wrapping an arm around her shoulders instead, and squeezed. "Well, I'm sorry for the pressure. I'm so glad to meet you I'm clearly running away with myself. Come on. There's a nice bottle of Chardonnay chilling in the fridge. How 'bout we go uncork it, hmm?"

* * *

Two hours later, Gram had Mandy ensconced on the living room sofa surrounded by no less than four picture albums. The old-fashioned rose-printed fabric on the sofa brought up childhood memories. Maybe it was an old-lady thing, but her own grandmother had had one exactly like it. Gram, though, seemed to have an affinity for roses. The sofa matched the pendulum clock on the wall over the fireplace, and several paintings containing yet more pink roses hung on the walls.

After dinner and dessert, Marcus had offered to do the dishes, and Gram had ushered her into the living room. Gram, it seemed, was a natural storyteller, because she hadn't stopped regaling Mandy with stories from Marcus's child-hood.

"Ahh, there he is in his Little League uniform." Gram's voice filled with pride as she tapped the open page on her lap. "Adorable, wasn't he?"

Mandy shifted her gaze to the album. In the picture Gram pointed at, Marcus couldn't have been more than ten or twelve. Tall and gangly, he stood with his team, all of them in bright orange shirts, white pants, and matching orange socks. He looked so different from the serious man she'd come to know. His dark hair was long enough that despite his baseball cap, the sides flopped over his ears, and his wide grin spread nearly from one ear to the other. It was the most expression she'd ever seen on his face. He didn't smile like that anymore.

She ran the tip of her index finger over his image, tracing his features. "Was he any good?"

Gram laughed softly. "Lord, no. Bless his heart, Marcus

couldn't hit the broad side of a barn, though his coach used to tell me there wasn't a more enthusiastic player on the team."

Gram turned the page and stopped, sitting silent for a moment.

"He was always good with tinkering, though. That's my rose clock, the same one up on the wall over there. I've had that thing for years. Bought it at a yard sale. It stopped working one year. Marcus fixed it for me. He used to love taking stuff apart, just to see how it worked. So every time one of my electronics stopped working, I'd give it to him, just to take apart. He fixed half of them."

Gram looked up from the photo album, peering across the room as Marcus came to stand in the doorway. He folded his arms and leaned against the frame, simply watching them. The expression on his face was hard to read, and it scattered her nerves. Did he know her stomach was tied in sickening knots? Meeting Gram and listening to her stories had given her a peek at the intimate side of the man. Something she would admit only to herself that she desperately craved.

It also served as a painful reminder that, eventually, she'd have to give all this up. She'd have to give *him* up. The question was, how much of her heart would be left when it ended? And, more to the point, could she still do this, play the part of his girlfriend? Did she even want to anymore?

Gram patted the seat beside her. "Come sit. I was about to show her pictures of Ava."

Marcus finally pushed away from the wall and moved into the room. He tucked his fingers in his pockets as he came to stand in front of the coffee table. "Actually, I was thinking we should probably go. It's getting late, and we both have to work in the morning."

Gram glanced in the direction of the clock over the fireplace.

"Would you look at that? It's almost nine." She patted Mandy's knee. "I got so lost in the memories. I hope I haven't bored you. Marcus is always saying I tell the same stories over and over."

Mandy smiled, praying it didn't look as forced as it felt. One thing she *had* decided: she didn't like having to lie to this sweet woman. A woman she was dying to get to know better. "Not at all. I enjoyed it. It was nice to see how he grew up. Thank you. For dinner, and, well, everything. He talks about you all the time, and it was so nice to finally meet you."

Gram pulled Mandy in for a tight hug. "You as well. Don't be a stranger. We should have lunch sometime. I can teach you to make those cookies."

"I'd like that." Mandy nodded, forcing the words out past the growing lump in her throat. She'd meant that. Probably more than she should.

Firmly ignoring the thoughts—and the twinge to her chest they inspired—she pushed off the sofa and crossed the room. What she wanted to do was get in the car and go home. She had a big decision to make. Namely, could she let this play out for another three weeks? All the while knowing she was only going to fall deeper for both of them?

She forced herself to stop beside Marcus, steeling herself for the assault on her senses he always was. The woodsy, earthy aroma that seemed to cling to him hit her nostrils first. The warmth and strength of his body next. She ached to wrap her arms around him, rest her head against that broad chest and listen to the soothing thump of his heartbeat, but she kept her hands to herself.

Marcus turned his gaze to where Cammie lay curled up on a blanket on the sofa beside Gram. "Time to go. Say goodbye."

Cammie rose to her feet, took a moment to stretch this way and that, then licked Gram's arm and hopped off the couch, trotting to his side.

Gram walked them to the door and hugged them both, bent to scratch Cammie's head and, like Mandy's mother always did, stood watching until they were in the car before closing the front door. As soon as she and Marcus were finally alone, the tension mounted. She hadn't a clue what to say to him anymore. She'd agreed to do this. Hell, it had been her idea. But the thought of continuing was a knot in her chest. She didn't know if she had to the strength to wrap herself up any further in his life. She hadn't counted on liking him or his grandmother. Hadn't expected their lives to fit quite so easily. It was only supposed to be a fling. Great sex with a guy she'd wanted since she met him.

Except all this evening had done was make her yearn for the thing she'd never have: his heart. He'd made that perfectly clear from day one. Marcus didn't do commitment.

The drive back to his place was too silent. Marcus stared out the windshield, concentrating on the road. She was trying not to think about what had to happen when they got home.

He blew out a breath and tossed a glance her way as he

changed lanes and headed for the highway exit. "All right, I can't stand it. You've been unusually quiet tonight. It's not like you. What's wrong? I thought that went well."

The details of tonight's dinner played through her mind, painful and heartwarming all at the same time. As usual for this time of year in the Northwest, rain picked up out of nowhere. Big fat drops slowly filled the glass. With each one, her heart sank further into the pits of her stomach. Truth was, she knew what she had to do.

She swallowed past the growing lump in her throat. "It did. I had a great time."

The heat of his stare burned into her, but Mandy couldn't force herself to look at him. She had no desire to look into those hypnotic eyes or see the connection she knew she'd find there. The one that would pull her deeper.

"And?" When she didn't elaborate, he sighed and settled a hand on her knee. His voice softened. "Angel, talk to me."

The term of endearment wrenched at her chest. The truth stared her in the face, like a giant neon sign, all lit up and blinking in the road ahead of them. It said, "Don't do this." If she wanted anything left of her heart at all, she'd do what was best for *her*. She'd already broken her promise to him, had broken rule number one—no emotion.

She wrapped her arms around herself and turned her head, watching the trees and house lights blur past. "I don't think I can do this anymore."

"Can't do what?" Suspicion and caution edged his voice.

This time, she forced herself to look at him. "Don't make me do this in the car."

He came to a stop at a red light and stared for a beat, then nodded and pulled his hand back.

The rest of the drive was eerily silent. Too much time for her to think, for doubt to insert itself into every corner of her mind. Was this really the right thing to do?

By the time he pulled into his driveway and shut off the engine, she could no longer be certain of anything. Only that she loved him. It would only get worse if she didn't extract herself from his life now.

Marcus, it seemed, had other ideas. After exiting the car, he took a moment to get Cammie out of the backseat and set her on the ground, then grabbed Mandy's hand and pulled her up the front walk. His fingers tightened almost painfully around hers as he unlocked the door. Was he afraid she'd bolt?

He shoved the front door open, waited as Cammie trotted off into the living room, before pulling Mandy inside. He didn't give her a chance to say anything. Rather he closed the door and rounded on her, pressing her back against the foyer wall, slid his hands in her hair, and sealed his mouth over hers. His lips all but bruised hers with the ferocity of his kiss. His tongue thrust into her mouth, restless and demanding.

Beneath the sheer power of him, Mandy caved. A quiet whimper escaped and her hands sought him in turn, sliding up his chest. She had to give him up, to end this tonight while some part of her heart still remained intact, but she wanted one more time with him. Wanted his scent imbedded in her skin, in her clothing, to lull her tonight when she had to go home alone and sleep without him.

When she lifted onto her toes, giving back everything he

gave her, Marcus groaned. He gripped her ass in his hands, and reminiscent of that night in Gabe's bathroom, lifted her off her feet and pressed her back against the door. Her skirt bunched around the tops of her thighs. Marcus shifted her weight, holding her with one arm as he shoved the material up over the curve of her ass. Then he reached between them and tugged open his fly.

Mandy reached down and pulled her panties aside, and with a flick of his hips, he pushed into her, sliding into her in one slick, ruthless thrust. His glorious, thick cock buried deep, and Mandy cried out as every sensitive nerve ending came alive. Never in a million years would she tire of this. His incredible passion, the absolute bliss of him filling her.

He wasn't slow or tender, either. No, he began a punishing rhythm, his hips pistoning into her, driving up into her hard. Every thrust shoved her ass into the wall behind her. Her breasts bounced, making her taut nipples rub his chest. God, it was bliss.

Mandy locked her legs around his hips and gave back with equal force. Their bodies came together with a ferocity that left her breathless, and every merciless thrust sent her careening toward oblivion. She welcomed it. In what could only have been a few dozen strokes, he struck that delicious match deep inside. Her orgasm burst through her, a luscious shower of hot sparks that left her shaking and moaning.

Marcus dropped his forehead onto her shoulder with a low groan. He thrust deep once, twice, and began to tremble as his own orgasm claimed him.

When the spasms finally ended, Mandy wrapped her

arms tightly around his shoulders and buried her face in his neck.

"You promised me a month."

Marcus's words came muffled from the vicinity of her throat.

Mandy tightened her grip on his shoulders, inhaled and filled her lungs. He deserved better, but she couldn't look at him when she said the words or the expression in his eyes would break her. She'd never get the words out. "I'm sorry. I know I did. But I can't do this with you anymore, Marcus. I just can't."

He attempted to pull back enough to meet her gaze. When she wouldn't release him, he growled in frustration. "Damn it, Mandy. Look at me."

She gave in and finally lifted her head. One look at his eyes, though, and she could no longer hold back the tears.

His jaw set in determination. "Why? You owe me that much."

"Please. Let me go." When she pushed against his chest, Marcus set her on her feet. She took a moment to straighten her skirt.

Marcus pulled up his jeans but didn't bother buttoning them. Instead, he gripped her chin in his palm, forcing her gaze back to his. His brow furrowed, but she didn't miss the panic in his searching eyes. Nor the way his chest rose and fell at a rapid pace. "Stop stalling, damn it, and tell me what the hell is going on."

"I like her. Do you know your grandmother offered to teach me to cook? We chatted in the kitchen while I helped her with the dessert and coffee. She told me that the chicken and dumplings she made was one of your favorites, and I made an offhanded comment about how I couldn't cook to save my life." All the fight drained out of her. She dropped her hands to her sides, her shoulders heavy. "I can't look that wonderful woman in the face and lie to her. It's killing me."

He shook his head, his gaze searching her face for a long moment. Finally, he dragged a hand through his hair and stepped back. "That's what this is? We're not exactly lying to her. More like...stretching the truth. We *are* seeing each other. And after last week, that's exactly what this is. Short-lived, maybe, but—"

"I failed my end of the bargain." Her heart hammered in her ears, but the truth stared her in the face. She owed it to him to be completely honest with him. She blew out a defeated breath, her voice lowering with the vulnerability rising over her. "I swore I could do this, but I didn't count on actually getting to know you. I just expected it to be really great sex, but..."

She shook her head and dropped her gaze to the floor, the rest of her words trailing off into the unbearable silence hanging over them.

This time, he didn't touch her, but ducked down to look into her face. "But what, angel?"

That word, that single term, nearly broke her. Her chest tightened until she thought it would crack wide open. She swallowed hard and forced herself to hold his gaze, but one look into those intense, beautiful eyes and the words came tumbling out, unstoppable.

"I'm in love with you, and I can't pretend I want just your friendship anymore. All tonight did was prove to me that I don't. I want more. I want it all. I want every Sunday with your grandmother, and I want to spend every night wrapped in your arms, from now until the foreseeable future. I want you to call me your girlfriend and be proud of it, and God help me, I want you to be able to tell me you love me, too, someday."

By the time she finished, her chest was heaving, her breaths coming in short, ragged pants. All she could do was wait for the fallout.

Marcus's eyes widened. His mouth opened and closed a few times, but no sound came out. Finally, he swallowed, his Adam's apple bobbing. "Angel . . ."

Mandy held up a hand. "Don't. Please. If you care about me at all, you won't say it. It wasn't intentional, wasn't something I set out to do. I just sort of ended up here. And I can't spend the next three weeks pretending this isn't killing me, or spending time with your grandmother and pretending I wouldn't kill to be a part of that. A real part. She's a wonderful person, you know, and when I told her I'd love to spend more time with her, I meant it. Which was what made me decide I couldn't do this anymore. Ironic, right?"

She let out a quiet laugh, the sound stark and grave. Her gaze went unfocused for a moment before she fixed it on him again.

"I'll just go." She didn't give him a chance to respond. She didn't want to hear it. If he uttered the words moving behind his eyes, if he told her—again—that he couldn't, or God forbid, that he didn't love her, too, it would crush her.

So she opened the door and forced herself to move outside to where her car was parked beside his in the driveway. As she climbed behind the wheel, the unbearable silence settled over her and a twinge of pain tightened her chest.

If this was the right thing to do, why did it feel so awful?

CHAPTER FOURTEEN

Marcus glared at his reflection in the bathroom mirror as he cinched the noose around his neck. It had taken him three tries to get the knot in this godforsaken tie even semi straight. All because he couldn't stop thinking about the funeral in two hours.

Somehow, he had to get through it alone. He might have convinced himself he was fine if it weren't for this damn suit. God, he hated these things. The black color reminded him of the masquerade on the Fourth of July. His first official date with Mandy.

He missed her. Goddammit. Missed her smile and her flirtatious laugh, when her eyes filled with mischief. When she knew damn well she'd cornered him and looked at him like a cat toying with a mouse.

He missed her body in bed beside him the most. Sleeping wrapped in her warm, soft curves, with that fluffy hair of hers in his face. Sad part was, he hadn't even realized he'd enjoyed it until it wasn't there anymore. Until *she* wasn't there anymore. Her absence had left a void in his life.

Today's funeral reminded him too much of the day they'd buried Ava. Four and a half years might have passed, but it felt like only yesterday. And he could use a bit of whatever the hell it was about Mandy that calmed him. Because he could deny it all he wanted, but she did. She'd righted his world.

Today of all days he needed her. Hell, it was a selfish thing to even think. Today wasn't about him. Except he understood, in a very personal way, what Jason's wife would be feeling, the denial as you stood beside a grave some part of you insisted you shouldn't be standing at for decades to come, the utter refusal to believe you'd never see your loved one again, and the desperate hope that you'd wake up to find it all a horrible dream. Then the slowly sinking realization that it wasn't.

He gave up on a perfect knot, sighed, and glanced down at his feet. Cammie had followed him in here, curled up and gone to sleep with her head resting against his bare toes. He bent and gently scooped her into the crook of his arm. "Come on, girl. Let's go see Gram."

She lifted her head, blinking sleepily at him.

He scratched behind her right ear. At least he wouldn't be completely alone today. "You miss Mandy, too, don't you girl?"

She licked his chin. One week and somehow, Mandy had managed to insert herself into his life. Even Cammie seemed to notice the absence. Every night when he came home, she'd come running to the door, and every night, she'd look past him, as if expecting someone else. The disappointment on her little face was palpable. She'd done the same thing for months after Ava died. Anybody who said dogs couldn't speak clearly wasn't paying attention.

"Yeah." He smoothed a hand over her soft head. "Me too."

The question now was, what the hell did he want to do about it? He'd been pondering *that* question since the door closed behind her.

With a sigh, he tucked Cam in one arm and headed for the front door, pocketed his keys, and headed out to his car.

Ten minutes later, he pulled into Gram's driveway. The knot in his gut tightened as he got Cammie out of the car. He still hadn't told Gram about Mandy. He wasn't looking forward to disappointing her.

He barely stepped up onto the porch when the front door opened. Gram scanned him from head to toe, worry wrinkling her brow. Two seconds later, she took him by the arm and pulled him inside, shutting the door behind him. Little creases formed around her mouth as she reached up, undoing the knot in his tie. "You've been tying these since you were twelve."

So she was starting with idle chitchat. That only meant one thing: a fishing expedition.

He rolled his eyes. She'd probably cuff him for it, but he wasn't in the mood today. "You were never very good at subtle, Gram. Whatever it is, just ask. I had a long night last night."

That strong blue gaze flicked to his. She studied him for a moment before dropping his tie and planting her hands on her hips. "All right, Mr. Grumpy. I'm worried about you. Today especially. And how come Mandy isn't here? I thought for sure she'd be going with you."

His stomach sank and Marcus dragged a hand through his hair. Crap. He should've known she'd ask that. There was no use lying to her, either. He owed her the truth, but he'd hoped they wouldn't have to have this conversation until *after* the funeral. Apparently, he wasn't so lucky.

He dropped his hand, stuffing both in his pockets with a heavy sigh. "Mandy and I aren't seeing each other anymore."

Her stern expression fell from her face, to be replaced by exactly what he'd hoped not to see: more concern. She laid a hand against his chest. "I'm sorry, honey. How come?"

He averted his gaze to the right, idly watching as Cam burrowed beneath the blanket Gram always kept on the couch. Better than having to watch Gram's eyes when he spilled the story.

"Mandy and I were temporary." Heat flooded his face. Christ. What a thing to have to tell her. He might as well have told her he'd gotten arrested for having sex in public. A glance at her found her frowning in disapproval, too. Time to move on with this conversation. "I brought her over for dinner because I thought... hell, I thought it would make you happy."

If she was angry that he'd lied to her, he couldn't say he blamed her. It didn't help that her gaze scanned him again. Moments later, her expression softened. She picked up the ends of his tie and began to re-form the knot.

"You being happy makes me happy, sweetheart. I knew I sensed tension between you two on Sunday." She cinched the knot tight, straightened his tie, then patted his chest and turned to walk away. "Come on. I'll make coffee and you can tell me what happened. Then we'll see if we can fix this."

He watched her head in the direction of the kitchen. "I'm not sure it *can* be fixed, Gram."

God knew he wanted to fix it, though.

She waved a hand behind her as she disappeared around the corner. "Everything can be fixed, sweetheart. You taught me that."

Yeah. If only it were as simple as fixing the gears on her clock.

With a reluctant sigh, he followed. When he entered the kitchen, she was standing in front of the coffeemaker, the top already open. Marcus leaned back against the opposite counter. Regret tightened his chest. "I don't know about this one. She wants something I'm not sure I can give her."

In the middle of filling the brew basket with fresh coffee grounds, Gram paused and looked back at him. "What's that, sweetheart?"

He forced himself to meet her gaze, because what he needed right now was a dose of that calm guidance she was so good at. "A future."

He still had no idea if he'd be any damn good at a relationship. Shouldn't he want more for Mandy than that?

Gram studied him. Several moments ticked out in silence that only further tightened the knot in his gut. She pursed her lips, telling him she had a lot on her mind. So, he stuffed his hands in his pockets and waited. She'd tell him eventually.

Finally, she shook her head slowly. "Son, I'm going to tell you something I've been dying to tell you for years. Up until now, I've kept quiet, hoping you'd find your own way."

If that wasn't Gram in a nutshell. Bossy but doing it from the right place. He pulled his hands from his pockets and folded his arms, trying his best to get rid of his smile. "Since when have you ever held back saying what was on your mind?"

"Oh, hush." She waved a hand at him, but her eyes glinted with amusement as she stepped toward him. She laid a hand against his chest, head tipped back to peer up into his face. "Your mother was my daughter, and I loved her very much, but you know what? Her leaving you and Ava was her loss. Keeping people at a distance has only accomplished one thing. It made you a lonely soul. You want to know why I bug you about finding someone? That's it. Because it's written all over you, and it worries me. You've been afraid of being left since she dropped you here that morning thirty years ago. It's time to let it go."

She gave a firm nod and returned to the coffeemaker, filling it with water.

The question caught on his tongue as he watched her. He swallowed hard and forced himself to voice it, because if he didn't ask, he'd never know. "But how do I know I'll even be any good at this? I've been alone my whole life. Hell. Look where I come from. I don't want to hurt her. Or disappoint her."

Gram shot a glance over her shoulder, that quiet worry etching her gaze.

"You are what you choose to be, sweetheart." She turned back to the counter, pulling ceramic mugs from the cabinet. "It takes two things to make a relationship work. Love and desire. And I don't mean passion. I mean the desire to *make* it work. Relationships aren't easy. You love her, don't you? That's what this is all about, isn't it? You've finally fallen and you don't know what to do with yourself. I could see it in you Sunday night, the way you looked at her..."

Gram continued to ramble, but Marcus could only stand there and stare. Her quiet statement had lodged in his brain, setting his heart hammering. Son of a bitch. *Did* he love her?

Yet barely a breath later, the truth settled over him. It didn't come at all the way he'd always envisioned it, either. It wasn't an earth-shattering moment that made him break out in a cold sweat. Rather, it came as a quiet acceptance that blossomed in his chest, warm and right.

He let out a huff of a laugh and reached up to rub the back of his neck. "Yeah. Yeah, I suppose I do."

Gram's eyes lit up like a child's on Christmas morning, though to her credit, she pressed her lips together in a not-so-subtle attempt to hide her smile. "Good. Now go tell her that."

She didn't give him time to respond, but grabbed his arm again, tugging him all the way to the front door. She let go of him long enough to pull it open, then pushed him out onto the porch.

"Stop by the florist around the corner. Bring her a rose. Just one." Brow furrowed, she held up a finger. "Red. It's classic, and it's sweet. Then talk to her. Show her what you show me, that soft heart I know is in there. Go. Trust me."

She waved her hands at him, shooing him, and shut the door in his face.

* * *

Standing in the middle of the crowd gathered at the cemetery an hour later, Marcus stared at the coffin, his vision unfocused. It was an oddly beautiful day. A little chilly, but the sky was clear and blue and dotted with puffy white clouds. Despite the forecasters call for rain, the sun beat down on the back of his neck, warming his skin.

Several dozen people surrounded the grave, all of them dressed in black. Some were family members. Most were fellow vets who'd come to pay their respects. As Marcus listened to the pastor's prayer, memories bombarded him. A similar funeral four years ago. Standing in the same basic spot the widow now stood in—beside an open grave, staring at a casket he kept praying was empty.

He turned his head, seeking out the widow. He didn't know her, had only met her a handful of times, but he understood what she was going through. She held herself well, all things considered. She wasn't a sobbing mess, but standing tall, with her shoulders pulled back. Had she moved beyond the shock and denial? Or had the realization kicked in? That this was real. That's when the life-altering grief would start. She'd have to go on, missing the one person who was supposed to always be there.

Not much had changed for him. He was still as alone today as he'd been four years ago. And as he watched the widow struggle to keep herself composed, one thought rose above the rest. He was tired of being alone. Tired of being that lone tree in the forest still standing. He wanted...shelter. Someone to have his back, to curl around at the end of every day.

Since Mandy ended their...hell. Relationship? Friendship? He didn't know what to call it. He only knew he missed her. After Ava's death, after spending his life watching people leave, he'd shut out the world. Hell. He'd shut down. Put his head down and focused on work. On getting through.

He'd thought he was doing all right until Mandy sauntered her way into his world. Now nights were god-awful lonely. And he couldn't deny it anymore. He wanted her. All of her.

Was Gram right? If he showed up at Mandy's apartment, would she even see him? Would she let him in? He certainly wouldn't, so why the hell should he expect her to? He'd let her leave.

The pastor concluded the prayer, and the crowd around him began to disperse. The widow stepped up to the casket, laid a white rose on top, bent to kiss the shiny wooden surface, then turned and walked away from the grave site.

With a resigned sigh, Marcus turned to head to where he'd parked his car at the edge of the grass. He needed to pick up Cam from Gram's, and then he'd go see Mandy. He hadn't a fucking clue how it would work, but he couldn't let her go now. If he had to earn her trust all over again, prove to her he had no intention of going anywhere...whatever. He'd do it. He'd scale a mountain for her. The question was, would she forgive him for being a blind fool?

He'd made it only a couple steps when a face among the crowd stopped him cold. Mandy. She stood not ten feet beyond him, wearing a black skirt suit. Had she been there the whole time? He blinked. Maybe she was a mirage.

She shrugged, one corner of her mouth hitching, but her wide-eyed gaze darted over his face. "I got here late. I didn't want to interrupt."

The relief that flooded him made him want to beat his damn chest. Or fall to his knees at her feet. He *wanted* to run over there and swoop her up, but he forced himself to remain calm as he moved toward her. "You came."

Something soft and vulnerable flitted across her features, there and gone too fast for him to be sure he'd seen it. She dropped her gaze to the grass, shifted from one foot to the other. After a moment, she looked up again. "I promised you I would."

Marcus halted halfway to her, stunned by the simplicity of her admission. Despite how they'd left things on Sunday, she'd come anyway. She'd set her own needs aside. For him.

She humbled him.

He resumed his trek, forcing himself to move slowly. He wanted to capture her face in his hands and kiss her breathless. None of which he could do. At least not yet. "I wouldn't have held it against you if you didn't, you know."

As he came to a stop in front of her, she tipped her head back to peer up at him. He didn't miss the rapid rise and fall of her chest, but Mandy squared her shoulders and held his gaze all the same. "I know, but I don't go back on my promises just because the timing's not perfect."

Her scent blew in on a breeze, that soft vanilla wafting past his nose, and only sheer force of will kept him from reaching out to her. "That's it? You came because you made a promise?"

She shrugged again, half-hearted and dismissive. "This isn't about me. I knew this would be difficult for you, and I'd never forgive myself if I didn't."

"You're an amazing woman, you know that? It means a lot to me that you're here."

He stopped just shy of telling her she was right, that he needed her, and stuffed his right hand in his pocket, fingering his keys.

"Are you busy for the next hour or so?" When her shoulders tensed, he picked up her hand and stroked his thumb across her soft knuckles. "I have a lot of things I want to tell you, but this isn't the right place. Have coffee with me. It won't take long."

Hell. He'd never bared his heart before, and talking might very well get him nowhere. She could still decide he wasn't worth the risk. If he didn't at least say the words, though, he'd regret it, and he already had a lot of regrets. Damned if he'd let her be one of them.

She sighed, her fingers relaxing in his. "All right. I have about an hour before my next client meeting. I drove here, so I'll have to meet you."

He jerked his gaze to hers, heart hammering in his ears. "Thank you. There's a Starbucks not far from here. That okay?"

She nodded. "I recall passing it on the way here. That's fine."

"Thank you. For what it's worth, it means a lot to me that you came." He kissed her cheek and squeezed her fingers, then forced himself to release her. "I'll meet you there."

* * *

Ten minutes later, they sat at a small table in a corner of the Starbucks. Marcus leaned back in his seat, taking in every gorgeous nuance of Mandy, seated across the table from him. The coffee shop around them was in full swing, no less than a dozen people in various states of acquiring and consuming coffee. He was attempting to gather his thoughts, to plan what he wanted to tell her, but the right words eluded him. His mind had gotten stuck on how important this was.

Oh, they'd made idle chitchat as they stood in line, ordering their drinks. Black for her and a vanilla latte for him. She'd teased him about his girly coffee. He'd forced a laugh. The entire conversation had been awkward and painful. Once relatively alone with her at their semi-secluded table, his mouth had gone dry.

Coffee trapped between both hands, Mandy turned her gaze out the window as she took another sip. "Do you plan to tell me what you brought me here for or am I going to have to play the guessing game?"

He reached up to the rub the back of his neck. "Sorry. I'll admit I'm nervous."

She turned her head, her brows furrowing. "*You're* nervous? Why?"

"Because I'm too aware our entire relationship is riding on

me finding the right words, and I'm not sure I have them." He scanned the coffee shop around them. "I'm not even sure this is the best place for this, but I was afraid if I invited you over, it would give you the wrong impression. That I was inviting you over for a booty call."

She set her coffee cup on the table. "Okay. You have my attention. What do you want to tell me?"

Crap. The moment of truth. His hand shook so bad he feared he'd drop his cup in his lap and spill hot coffee all over his groin. Wouldn't that make a lasting impression?

He drew a deep breath to calm his scattered nerves, but as he met her gaze again, an odd sense of peace settled over him. He didn't know a lot of things right then, but whatever happened after this, he could never be sorry he'd told her.

He set his hands on his thighs. "I'm in love with you."

Several moments passed in unbearable silence. His stomach tightened. His palms sweat. Hell, warmth prickled along his skin, making his suit and tie more than a little stifling. Like the heat in the coffee shop had gone up twenty degrees. Mandy sat and stared, eyes widened slightly and searching his face, mouth hanging open. He was dying to know what she thought, but he fisted his hands in his lap and forced himself to wait her out.

Finally, she leaned back in her chair and folded her arms. "The night we agreed on a fling, you told me commitment wasn't your thing. That if I was looking for something more than fleeting, that wasn't you." One shoulder hitched, nonchalant, but those shrewd eyes pinned him to his seat. "What's changed?"

He smiled. Out of everything she could have asked, that was easy. "Me. I missed you."

A soft flush rose into her cheeks. Mandy diverted her gaze out the window again, but that quiet vulnerability she was good at moved over her. Marcus took her silence as encouragement. Maybe he was getting to her. So he went on.

He leaned forward, folding his hands on the table. "Frankly, I hadn't expected that, but the last three days have been hell. I hate that you're not mine anymore. That I can't touch you or kiss you simply because I feel like it. From now on, whenever the gang gets together, I'll have to go back to treating you like you're just Trent's kid sister. And don't get me started on where my head goes when I think of you with someone else."

Mandy looked over at him. Amusement glinted in her eyes. "Where *does* it go?"

"Down a violent path." His knee bounced beneath the table as the thoughts filled his head all over again. He'd pondered it a lot. Her with someone else. Running into her somewhere, or God forbid, that she'd actually fall in love and bring one of them to a get-together. "Frankly, thinking about it makes me want to rip his head off and shove it up his ass."

A quiet laugh burst out of Mandy. "You always were one-part caveman, Marcus."

"But I'm your caveman, angel. And so we're clear, I don't want to be just your friend anymore, either. I want it all. I have to be honest, though. I can't guarantee I'll even be any good at a relationship. I've never had one before. Not like this."

Mandy sat blinking at him for a moment. "Because I'm different."

The exact conversation she referenced filled his mind. That night when they'd agreed to a fling. He shrugged. "I know you don't believe me, but you are. I've never felt this way about someone before. Gram was right. My life is good, but it's empty. Funny thing is, it wasn't until you walked away that I realized it. You're that rare sunny day, after months and months of nothing but gray skies and rain. You're bright and beautiful and I have no desire to let you go."

Marcus set his hand on the table palm up. Mandy hesitated before tentatively placing her hand in his, and he closed his fingers around hers. Vulnerability moved over him, making his stomach knot. Only with her could he let his guard down like this, but right then, with so much riding on him finding the right words, it still left him feeling naked and exposed. His belly laid bare.

"I needed you today. It feels like it was only yesterday I was standing at Ava's funeral, wishing like hell I'd wake up from whatever nightmare I was trapped in. I was watching that guy's wife. It was odd, like seeing myself from someone else's eyes. I could see her struggle with the same things I did, and it just brought it all back. And to have to do it without you?"

He followed the lines in her palm with the tip of his index finger. Mandy didn't say anything. So he went on, before he lost the nerve to say the words.

"I hated that you weren't there. That I'd fucked this up to the point that a friendship between us would never work. But

God, I wanted you there. You were all I thought about the whole damn time." He shook his head slowly as the memory of the funeral filled his thoughts. "And then I turned around and there you were. Like an angel from heaven. I have to tell you, it took a lot of willpower not to wrap myself around you and plaster my mouth on yours right there in front of everybody."

There it was. All laid out neat and tidy. Marcus drew a cleansing breath and forced himself to look at her. Mandy sat watching him, her expression surprisingly soft and open.

"I had to. I knew how painful it would be for you, and I knew I'd never forgive myself if I let this"—she waved a hand between them—"become more important than the promise I made you. It wasn't about me."

He laughed. "And that right there is *why* I love you and one of the reasons I want this. You put your own needs aside. For me. So you should know, angel, I'm not letting you go."

The corners of her mouth twitched, amusement blossoming in her eyes. She raised her brows, once again that sassy, spunky woman who didn't hesitate to put him in his place. "I don't get a say in this at all?"

Relief flooded his insides. That she was teasing him had to be a good sign. He probably shouldn't voice the words seated on his tongue, but her smile lightened his load by a lot, and damned if he could resist.

"Nope. If you need time to learn to trust me again, to trust that I mean it when I say I'm not going anywhere, I'm okay with that. I have all the time in the world to wait you out. But you're mine, angel, and I'm not giving you up." He set his other hand on the table, palm up. More than anything, he wanted her to know he was serious. "I'm yours, Mandy. For as long as you'll have me. I suppose the question now is, will you?"

As he waited for her response, his heart shot up into his throat, and his whole body tensed. He hoped she'd take his hands again. She'd come to the funeral, so clearly she still cared, but had he pushed her too far?

Instead of taking his hand, Mandy got up from the table and propped her free hand on her hip. "Grab your coffee, sailor."

When he stood and did as ordered, Mandy picked up his hand and pivoted, her heels *click-clack*ing on the tiled floors as she marched from the coffee shop, tugging him behind her. She strode outside and through the small parking lot, to where she'd parked her car in the back. She stopped beside the driver's door and faced him again. "I just didn't think a full Starbucks was the right place to do this."

He furrowed his brow. "To do what?"

She braced her hands against his chest, rose onto her toes, and sealed her mouth over his.

Marcus groaned. Her mouth was soft and warm and familiar, and in seconds flat, he was putty at her feet and melting into her. Her lips plied his like she had all the time in the world. When she finally came back up for air, he was breathing hard. From arousal. From nerves. His only saving grace was that Mandy's chest rose and fell to the rapid pounding of his heart. Her warm breaths puffed against his skin.

She leaned into him, chest to chest, hip to hip, and stared him dead in the eye. "I want."

Relief flooded his chest.

"Minx." He tucked that errant curl behind her right ear and took a moment to simply enjoy the feel of her there. She was his, and it humbled him. "You scared the hell out of me. I wasn't sure if you were accepting or sending me off."

She let out a quiet laugh. "Sorry. I couldn't help myself. You're cute when you're nervous." Her expression sobered. "You didn't really think I'd say no, did you?"

He shrugged. "When you left Sunday night, I had every intention of leaving well enough alone. I just didn't expect to miss you so much. But I still let you leave."

She smiled, soft, alluring, and leaned closer. Until her mouth hovered a bare inch over his and her warm breaths teased his skin all over again. "Sometimes, all a girl really wants is to know that you love her, too."

He brushed his mouth over hers, a sense of vulnerable honesty creeping through him. Only with her. "Then I'll say it again. I love you."

She sipped at his mouth, the barest, lightest kiss, and grinned. "Good. I love you, too."

He lifted a hand, traced the curve of her face, tucking that willful curl at her temple behind her ear. "I have to be honest, though. I meant it when I said I'm no good at this. Gram tells me I can be moody, and when things get tough, I have a tendency to bottle it up. There may be times when I shut you out without meaning to." He touched his nose to hers and lowered his voice. "Promise me you won't let me."

Her brow furrowed. "I don't expect you to be perfect. I fell in love with you because you're intense and passionate. You accept me for who I am, make me feel beautiful and like the only woman in the room. You've also helped me realize that there's nothing wrong with me exactly the way I am. I like football and cars. So what?"

He touched his nose to hers. "Far as I'm concerned, you *are* the only woman in the room. And I'll say it again. Those guys who didn't want you are clueless idiots."

She let out a soft laugh.

He wrapped both arms around her. "You know, I guarantee you I'll make mistakes, angel."

"If you're trying to scare me away, it's not working. I'm not afraid of you." She winked at him, but just as quickly she sobered again. "We'll play it by ear, take it as comes."

"You are so goddamn gorgeous. Thank you. I honestly haven't thought much beyond this. Just that I want to spend as much time with you as I can." He brushed his mouth over hers, murmuring into the space between them, "Speaking of which...can I see you tonight?"

She smiled shyly, a soft flush in her cheeks. "I'd like that. Dinner?"

"My place." He raised his brows. "I'll cook. You bring the wine?"

"Deal." She leaned up onto her toes, kissing him again, this one soft and lingering, then set back down on her heels. She dropped her gaze, running the edge of his tie between her thumb and forefinger. "You know, I'm glad Military Match paired us up that night."

He smiled, heart light and full. "Me too. I almost didn't go. Putting on that monkey suit was almost a deal breaker for me."

Her soft laugh made his chest expand. God, how he loved that sound. He wanted to hear it often, would likely make an ass of himself to get her to laugh as often as he could.

"Well, I for one think you look fantastic in it. I have to go. I have a meeting in twenty minutes. I'll see you tonight. I'll stop by Lauren's bakery for some dessert as well." She pecked his lips and pulled her car door open, setting her purse and coffee inside. A bare breath later, she seemed to remember something because she turned back, brows raised. "Oh, did I tell you I talked to Trent about us last night?"

Marcus smiled and folded his arms. "Did you, now? Well, guess what? You're mine and you'll always be mine, no matter what Trent thinks about it."

She laughed. "Good. Because he said I could do a lot worse than you." She winked, kissed his cheek, and climbed into her car. "See you for dinner."

He stared at her window, his mind processing. Mandy's car thrummed to life beside him as his thoughts finally settled on one point. Wait a minute . . .

He bent down and tapped on her window, waited until she rolled it down, and leaned on the edge. "What made you go talk to your brother?"

She grinned. A full-out, shit-eating, proud-of-herself grin. "Because I'd decided I wasn't giving you up either."

EPILOGUE

She looks beautiful, doesn't she?" Mandy sighed. She'd never stop being a hopeless romantic, and the sight before her was full-on dreamy. Five feet or so beyond her, Gabe and Steph swayed to the soft music playing from speakers set high on the walls.

The lovebirds had gotten married that afternoon. A small ceremony, close friends and family only. Now the reception was in full swing. Drinks flowed and a happy buzz floated through the room. The band played a slow, romantic number as the guests gathered around to watch them share their first dance as husband and wife.

Gabe leaned down and kissed Steph softly, and Mandy's heart hitched at the love shining between them. They were in a world all their own, and she couldn't be happier for the two of them. She'd been a nervous wreck making Steph's dress, but it had turned out beautiful. A simple design: ankle-length silk, delicate spaghetti straps, and accented by a crystal-studded belt. The gown cascaded over Steph's gorgeous hourglass figure. She looked perfect in it.

Marcus, standing quietly behind her up until now, slipped his arms around her waist, and bent his head to her neck. "Mmm. She looks beautiful, but I'm afraid I'm a bit biased. If you ask me, the most beautiful woman in this room is currently in my arms."

Heart lightened by his touch and his sweet words, she stroked her hand along the sleeve of his suit jacket and leaned her head back against his chest. "Glad to see you're in a good mood tonight. You haven't been yourself lately."

Over the past year, their relationship had become...comfortable, in a favorite pair of jeans sort of way. More often than not she stayed at his place. He'd call her at work and tell her to meet him at *home* when she finished for the day. Over dinner, they'd chat, and then they'd take Cammie for a walk. Every night he'd make love to her, passionate and intense as always, and every night she'd fall asleep wrapped tightly in his arms.

It was bliss. The closer Gabe and Steph's wedding got, though, the more distant he'd become. No matter how often she asked if something was wrong, he said no. Tonight's good mood hopefully meant that, whatever it was, he'd resolved it.

He stilled, then sighed and rested his chin on top of her head. "Sorry I've been so distant. I've been doing some thinking."

Crap. Was that good or bad? "About?"

He ducked his head. His voice rumbled in her ear, a low, husky murmur. "Steph's dress is gorgeous, but I think yours should be more like the one you wore to the masquerade. You looked beautiful in that dress."

She froze. Surely he wasn't saying what she thought he was..."What are you talking about?"

He nudged her earlobe with his nose. "Your dress."

Her heart beat so hard it became a dull thud in her ears. God, if he didn't get to the point soon, she'd expire right here. "My dress for what?"

He heaved a sigh. "Your wedding dress, angel."

She squeezed her eyes shut, forcing herself to draw a slow, deep breath. "Marcus Denali, don't toy with me."

They hadn't talked about the future. He never brought it up, and she was content with their relationship as it was. She couldn't deny, though, that helping Steph and Gabe with their wedding plans and creating Steph's dress had her dreaming of "what if." She loved Marcus more now than she had a year ago, when he'd sat across that Starbucks table, looked her in the eye, and told her he loved her. She couldn't imagine her life without him, and the way he held her at night told her he felt the same.

Now? Hell. She wasn't sure what he was telling her now.

Marcus heaved a sigh. "I'm not toying with you, angel, I promise, but clearly I'm not doing this right. Maybe I should be a bit more blunt."

She reached back, caressing his stubbled cheek. "That would really be nice, because I'm very confused."

He released her, moved around in front of her, and stared down at her for a moment, something somber in the depths of his eyes. The slight tremor in his fingers as he reached into the inside pocket of his suit jacket didn't escape her notice either. The last time she could remember him being this nervous was...well, that day in Starbucks.

He finally pulled his hand from his pocket and turned it over. Seated on his palm was a navy-blue jewelry box. One corner of his mouth hitched as he pried the lid open. Inside the velvet box sat a gorgeous ring. A single, traditional solitaire with a white-gold band twisted to resemble a knot beneath the setting. "Do you have any idea how hard it was to hide this from you?"

She stifled a gasp behind her hand, looking between him and the ring. "This? This is what you've been all secretive about? God, I thought..."

Her breathing hitched as the moment rushed up on her, and the rest of the words refused to leave her throat. All she could do was stare at Marcus's handsome face while the beautiful music for Steph and Gabe's first dance played in the background.

"Sorry, angel. I wanted it to be right, and I'm nervous as hell. I've never done this before." He cleared his throat and dropped to one knee in front of her. "Marry me, Mandy."

His form blurred before her as tears flooded her eyes. She reached out, slipping her fingers through his hair. "You scared the hell out of me. To quote someone I know, I wasn't sure if you were hinting at something or preparing to send me off."

"I told you this a year ago, and I'm sure I've told you every day since, but apparently you need to hear it again: I love you, and I'm never letting you go. I want forever, and I want it official." The box trembled in his palm, but his gaze remained steady on hers. "Say yes, angel."

A single tear slipped passed her defenses, trailing down her cheek. Marcus always insisted he wasn't good with words, that he wasn't good with relationships, but he couldn't be more wrong. He might be a man of few words, but the ones he spoke often left her speechless. Like now.

There were probably about a thousand things she ought to say to him in return. That she loved him with everything she had and everything she was. How grateful she was they'd found each other at the masquerade. Or even that the thought of spending the rest of her life with him filled her with an unparalleled sense of rightness, whether they actually got married or not.

As it was, the words caught in the lump in her throat, and all she managed was a whispered, "Yes."

Marcus launched to his feet, swooped her up, and crushed her against his chest. "You've just made me the happiest man on the planet."

Applause erupted throughout the room, several whistles piercing the air. She'd gotten so caught up in his proposal she hadn't even realized the music had stopped. She turned her head, taking in the crowd around them. Gabe and Steph now stood side by side within the circle, holding hands. Everyone else was staring at her and Marcus, and every face was smiling.

Lauren caught her eye and gave her a thumbs-up. Trent, standing behind Lauren, smiled. Warmth filled his eyes as he winked.

Her face heating a thousand degrees, Mandy turned toward Steph, ready to apologize for stealing her and Gabe's limelight, when Gabe looked to Marcus and cocked a dark brow.

"Took you long enough." A slow grin curled across Gabe's face. "We stalled as much as we could."

Marcus's cheeks turned a soft shade of pink as he rubbed the back of his neck. "Damn nerve-racking thing to do in the middle of a crowd."

Mandy frowned, looking to Gabe and Steph, who both stood with knowing grins. "Wait...you guys knew?"

Steph nodded, then made her way to Mandy, enveloping her in a brief hug. "He asked for my advice. I told him doing it tonight would be perfect. Gabe agreed."

Mandy laughed and shook her head, completely over-whelmed by it all. "Well, congratulations. You all surprised the hell out of me. Thought this was supposed to be your day?"

"Oh, I couldn't resist. It's romantic, and I knew you wouldn't be expecting it." Steph waved a hand at her and hugged her again. "Congrats, you."

Lauren announced her presence by wrapping her in a hug from behind. "I'm so happy for you."

Mandy pulled back, swiped a hand across her damp cheek, and looked to Lauren. "I suppose you were in on this, too?"

"Nope. This was all Steph." Lauren laughed, then turned to Marcus and nudged him with her hand. "Nice going."

"Thanks." He flashed a sheepish grin, cheeks still slightly pink, then tilted his head in Mandy's direction. "Any chance of me getting my girl back?"

"Of course." Steph flashed a warm smile.

Steph and Lauren hugged her again before everyone wandered off, leaving her and Marcus alone once again. The music resumed, and couples paired off around them. Marcus held out his hand. "How 'bout a dance, beautiful?"

She slipped her hand into his, letting him pull her close, then laid her head against his chest. "I love you, you know that?"

Marcus drew her the tiniest bit closer, until there wasn't a hairbreadth of space between them, and ducked his head, resting his cheek against her temple. His voice was warm in her ear. "I love you, too."

They danced in silence for a few moments before the urge to share became too strong to deny. He might as well know it all. "Marcus?"

"Mmm?"

"I should probably tell you now...I want kids."

He chuckled and pressed a kiss into her hair. "Gram will be very pleased to hear that."

She lifted her head, peering up at him. "And you?"

He brushed a soft kiss across her lips. "Me too."

DID YOU MISS LAUREN AND TRENT'S LOVE STORY?
THEN CHECK OUT *A SEAL'S COURAGE*, THE FIRST BOOK IN
JM STEWART'S SEXY MILITARY MATCH SERIES! SEE THE
NEXT PAGE FOR AN EXCERPT.

Chapter One

"I'm going to be a virgin until I die." Lauren Hayes let out a world-weary sigh and sank back against the plush leather seats. The club around her pulsed, the throbbing beat and surging bodies lending an upbeat atmosphere Lauren couldn't get into.

Stephanie Mason, one of her two best friends, peered over the rim of her drink, her straw dangling from the side of her mouth. "You need to give up your perfect-man wish list, babe, and settle for Mr. Right Now, because Mr. Right doesn't exist."

Lauren eyed the two women seated across the table from her and sighed. "I know it's old-fashioned, but I wanted my first time to be with someone who'd actually remember my name in the morning. Not some hookup in a bar."

Mandy Lawson, best friend number two, shook her head, sending her short dark curls swishing over her shoulder. "I'm afraid, sweets, as the saying goes, if you want to find Prince Charming, you have to kiss a few toads. You're not going to lose your virginity by being picky."

Mandy had been her best friend since junior high. They'd met in home ec when their teacher partnered them together for a project. She'd told Lauren long ago she was nuts for making that chastity pact in ninth grade. She and a few of the other girls from church promised to remain virgins until they married. At the time, Lauren had made it with good intentions. When she was ten, her birth mother died in a car accident while driving home from another date with yet another fling. Having a single mother who slept around so much she didn't even know who Lauren's father was had left a lasting impression. She'd grown up determined to never, *ever*, become like her mother.

Lauren waved a hand at Mandy. "Oh, I know, but it's hard to reconcile my ideas of how true love should be with the desire to lose my virginity as quickly as possible."

Lauren had strict rules for how she lived her life, things she'd gleaned from her adoptive mother, Mary. Mary had started out as her foster mother, eventually adopting her when she was eleven. She'd gotten lucky. Not all kids who ended up in foster care got adopted. Mary had been a deeply religious woman and had old-fashioned ideas, particularly when it came to things like dating and sex. Never make the first move. No kissing on the first date. No drinking or staying out late. Number one on that list? No sex before marriage.

The problem was, Lauren had yet to do much actual living. She had yet to know the gloriousness of sex. Or getting so drunk she woke up the next day not remembering how she'd gotten home. Or hell, the simple pleasure of making out with a guy. Wasn't most of that normal teenage behavior?

Mary had lived a safe—but boring—life. Her strict rules had kept her from living as much as she could have. She'd devoted herself to the church and to raising Lauren, and had died in her sleep, in her favorite recliner with her knitting in her lap. Mary's death had hit Lauren hard. And it had taught her one thing: life was short. She wanted to have a little fun before she died. To give up "the rules" and do all those things she'd held back on out of fear of doing the wrong thing. So far she hadn't done any of that.

She picked up her drink—some fruity concoction with sex in the name, courtesy of Steph—and took a sip before eyeing the girls again. "It's sad, isn't it? I'll be twenty-eight next week, and I've never even fallen in love. Infatuation, sure, and something that felt an awful lot like love until I realized it was one-sided."

Across the table, Stephanie waggled her blond brows. "Just do it, babe. Go dance, rub up against some hottie, and let nature takes its course."

Oh, she'd tried that. After Mary's death, she'd jumped into the dating pool, determined to get herself out there. She'd signed up for several of those dating sites and had gone on plenty of dates. The problem was, they never went anywhere. More than a few of the men wanted nothing to do with a virgin. Some had been a little *too* eager for her tastes. Most, though, had simply never called her back before she'd even gotten around to admitting that she was a virgin.

Lauren shook her head. "I agree it's time, but that's not me. Hell, I'd probably trip over my own feet and make a complete dork of myself."

She was born with the klutz gene. If she didn't watch the ground when she walked, she tended to trip over stuff. She couldn't count the number of times she'd run into a pole or another person because she'd been too wrapped up in her thoughts.

"You know..." Mandy, who was a little more down to earth, took a moment to gulp down the last of her beer. She set the bottle on the table and leaned forward to grin at Lauren. "I could always—"

"Oh, no." Lauren laughed and held up her hands. She didn't need to ask to know where this was going. Mandy loved playing matchmaker. "No way am I letting you fix me up again. You're a fabulous wedding designer, sweetie, but your taste in men sucks. There was Jake the octopus, who had eight arms and wouldn't take no for an answer. And then there was Guy, who talked about himself all night and how wonderful he was. Need I go on?"

Mandy's bottom lip popped out, but her cheeks flushed bright crimson. "Aw, come on. They weren't all awful. I know a hot military guy who'd be right up your alley..."

Lauren laughed again and jabbed a pointed finger at Mandy. "No."

"Actually..." Mandy looked to her left, flagging down the waitress and signaling for a refill by holding up her empty beer bottle. When the waitress smiled and nodded, Mandy turned back around and leaned her elbows on the table. "There's a new dating service I just heard of. You remember Jennifer Dillon, from high school?"

Lauren nodded. "Didn't I see an engagement announcement in the paper last week?"

"Yup. She and her fiancé came into my office the other day for help planning the wedding. In fact, I recommended your bakery for the cake. Ohhh, Laur, you should have seen her fiancé. He's air force. Tall, broad shouldered, and so polite. Came in dressed in his uniform, all 'yes, ma'am' and 'no, ma'am.'"

Lauren sipped at her drink. "No. I'm not letting you set me up again. I don't care if he's got a brother or friends or a million bucks."

Mandy furrowed her brow, glaring in disapproval. "Will you just listen? While we were talking about her wishes for the ceremony, I asked her where she'd met him. She said they used this service. Military Match. Kind of pricey, but the woman who runs it screens her applicants. So when I went home that night, I checked it out online." Mandy's blue eyes gleamed with impishness. "All the men are vets."

"Oh, I'm definitely in." Steph nudged Lauren with an elbow. "So are you."

Lauren couldn't stop the fierce heat that flooded her cheeks. These ladies knew her too well. Okay, she had to admit it. She had a "thing" for military men. There was something about a guy who willingly put his life on the line for people who couldn't fight for themselves. The uniform alone could melt her panties.

She sipped at her icy drink in a vain attempt to cool down. "I don't know what you're talking about."

Mandy laughed. "Right. Don't think I never noticed the way you'd go all tongue-tied whenever Trent came home on leave."

Steph turned her head, winking at Lauren. "Or the way you drool when he walks away from you."

Mandy was the youngest of three. Her brothers were ten years older than her and twins. Trent and Will might look identical, but the two couldn't be more different. Will was clean-cut. The guy in suits and ties rather than jeans and worn T-shirts. Trent had always been rough around the edges, a quiet guy who preferred to work with his hands.

A Navy SEAL, he'd gotten out of the service and returned home eighteen months ago with scars, some visible, some not. He now worked in a custom motorcycle shop doing detail work. Of the two brothers, Trent was the one who had always made her cream her panties. More to the point, Mandy knew she had a crush on him.

Steph looked over at Mandy. "How he's doing anyway?"

Mandy shook her head and sighed. "He's...different. He's always been quiet, but he crawled into himself after he came home and hasn't come back out yet."

Trent had post-traumatic stress disorder. Nightmares. Flashbacks. Coming home, he'd had a hell of a time of it. Mandy was right. He was doing better these days, but he still wasn't the guy he'd been before his last deployment.

Lauren dropped her gaze, pretending to be absorbed in her drink. "You should sign *him* up for that dating service. Might do him some good."

Mandy laughed. "Nope. He won't let me fix him up, either." Mandy rose to her feet and came around the table, tugging Lauren out of her seat. "Come on, ladies. Let's go find us some hotties and shake our tail feathers."

* * *

The following evening, Lauren pulled open her front door to find Mandy standing on her doorstep. She wore a sheepish grin Lauren had seen too many times over the years. It usually meant trouble.

Lauren folded her arms, narrowing her gaze. "All right. What did you do?"

Mandy's cheeks blazed bright red, and she took sudden interest in her sneakers. "I signed you up. I signed us all up, actually."

Lauren's heart took off on a one-hundred-meter dash. She had a sneaking suspicion she knew what Mandy referenced, but she needed to hear her headstrong best friend own up to it. "Signed us up for what?"

"That dating agency." Mandy looked up then, flashed a *please-don't-be-mad* grin, and clasped her hands together. "Steph's excited about it . . ."

Lauren's eyes widened. "Oh my God, Mandy. How could you do that? You don't know anything about this woman or this service."

"Actually, I do." Mandy stepped over the threshold, grabbed Lauren's wrist, and after closing the front door, pulled her into the living room. Once there, she took a seat on the sofa and patted the spot beside her. "I know I can be a little . . . impulsive, but I went to talk to the woman. She won't let me sign you up officially until you come down to speak to her yourself. Laur, you'd like her. Turns out, Karen's husband works with Trent at the bike shop. She's really down to earth and sweet. She's a great big romantic, but she's strong minded, like you. She wants her clients to feel comfortable with their experience, whether it lasts or not."

Lauren dropped onto the sofa beside her. Okay, so she was impressed Mandy hadn't rushed headlong into this, but she had enough experience with Mandy not to let her off the hook yet. "You should've consulted me first."

Mandy nudged her with an elbow. "Come on. You know you would've said no. Besides." Mandy dropped back against the sofa cushions with a tired sigh. "Jennifer was so happy when she came into my office the other day. I mean glowing. So is Skylar. The expression on her face when she looks at Will? I've never seen him so calm or so happy. I want that. One guy who makes me feel feminine and beautiful, who isn't turned off by the fact that I can take care of myself. Clearly I won't find it on my own."

Lauren leaned back and lay her head against Mandy's. "Me, either."

Mandy reached for her hand. "So do this with me. Us. Go talk to Karen and decide for yourself. You're right, you know. You shouldn't lose your virginity to some jerk you meet in a bar. Or in the back of a Toyota like I did."

Lauren blew out a heavy breath. "Fine. I'll talk to Karen, but that's all I'm promising you for now."

Mandy was right about one thing: since Mary's death, she'd been thinking about pushing herself beyond her comfort zone.

Mandy threw her arms around Lauren's shoulders and squeezed gently. "You won't regret it, Laur, I promise."

Lauren laughed softly. "I sincerely hope not."

* * *

Lying in the darkness of her bedroom, Lauren stared at the shadowy ceiling above her. A glance at the clock told her it was just past nine. She needed to be sleeping. After all, she had to be up at three, so she could be at the bakery by four. But no matter how many times she closed her eyes, sleep wouldn't come.

All because she'd gone over to see Trent tonight. Steph's casual mention of him two nights ago had inspired the worry.

For the longest time after he'd come home, Trent's PTSD had meant he'd barely left his apartment, even to fill his fridge. It's what had worried his family so much and why she'd taken to going over to see him on a regular basis. She'd wanted to help. A decision to bring him food one night had launched a thousand arguments and a thousand conversations.

Over the last year, he'd become a friend. She'd gone over to check on him one night after work, nine months ago now. Bringing him meals he could keep in the fridge and heat up later had always just been an excuse. She'd expected him to be his usual grumpy self, that he'd glare at her and tell her to leave. It's what he always did. She'd barge into his apartment—because she'd been instructed not to take no for an answer—and he'd follow her around as she made him a meal or cleaned and complain about her "invading his damn house."

This particular time, though, he'd actually invited her to stay. Ever since, it had become a tradition. Once or twice a week, she'd take him a meal or two, and he'd invite her to have dinner with him.

So it had been when she'd gone to see him after work today.

They'd sat and chatted about their days while chowing down on the lasagna and garlic bread she'd brought over.

Now, hours later, she couldn't sleep because she couldn't stop seeing his smile. Being a serious man, he didn't smile often, but when he did, he was downright magnificent. It transformed his whole face. Harsh, cut features softened, and his cobalt-blue eyes lit up like the sun.

God, she swore she'd gotten over her crush on him in high school. After all, he'd gotten married and had gone overseas, and she'd grown up and moved on. But since he'd come home, those scintillating feelings had begun to sneak up on her again. Except Trent was now divorced. Single. And that solitary fact teased her senses. Her body didn't seem to care that he tended to treat her like she was another sister. That he didn't seem to see her as a woman.

No, she always came away from time with him more aroused than she knew what to do with. Trent was every woman's dream. Polite. Charming. Funny. A hard worker. And it all came in a rock-hard package. God help her, he'd become her naughty little secret.

Even now the addicting rumble of his laugh echoed through her mind, shivering down her spine and landing straight in her panties. He'd teased her about her need to clean whenever she came over. It had started as an excuse to stay, to force him to interact, but had long since become a nervous habit.

Tonight he'd bumped her shoulder and laughed, and that one simple contact lit her body on fire. Because lately she couldn't help imagining what that hard body of his would feel like pressed against hers.

Giving in to the pull, she closed her eyes and slipped her hand inside her panties. Already hot and wet, a single glide over her swollen clit sent a heated shiver running through her. Her breathing hitched as her mind filled with the now familiar fantasy. Her favorite. The heat of his body against hers. His hot mouth skimming her neck, her shoulder, her ear. Teasing her sensitive skin. He'd slip those wonderfully long, warm fingers into her panties, massage her aching clit.

It was so real, she swore she could feel the hot huff of his breath in her ear. The calluses on the tips of his fingers. All too quickly, the luscious, achy pressure built. Heat prickled along her skin, and her inner muscles began a rhythmic squeezing, tightening and loosening. She rocked her hips into her hand, all the while imagining her fingers were his. Massaging. Circling. Driving her out of her mind with their ability to send her careening toward bliss at breakneck speed.

It didn't take long. Just the thought of him had made her so hot a few flicks over her engorged clit pushed her over the edge. Her orgasm tore through her, a luscious, hot bubble that burst inside of her. She massaged through every blinding pulse, determined to make it last as long as possible.

When the luscious spasms finally subsided, she collapsed back onto the bed and opened her eyes, lying there a moment, limbs deliciously heavy, while attempting to regain control over her breathing. The shadowy ceiling came back into focus, and the quietness of the house seeped around her.

The unbearable loneliness crept up right behind it. The way it always did. The one thing missing in this scenario was the warm, masculine body against her side. She longed for the pleasure to have been shared and for strong arms to hold her while she slept, and their lack left an emptiness deep inside.

Now, staring up at her ceiling, all she could see were the similarities between her and Mary. Mary had been a sweet woman with a heart of gold. She'd given Lauren a good life and had made her feel loved. But Mary had never been willing to take risks, had never put herself out there. And then she'd died alone, never having found her true love. What if Lauren ended up the same way?

Determination expanded inside of her. She pulled her hand from her panties and moved into the attached bathroom. After relieving herself and washing her hands, she strode down the hallway and into the kitchen. There on the counter sat the notepad she wrote her grocery list down on. She pulled it close, grabbed the pen beside it, and started making a list of all the things she'd never done but had always wanted to.

1: Lose my virginity

She paused, frowning down at the pad. Accomplishing number one would require finding the guy first, though.

Her conversation with Mandy two evenings ago came flooding back.

Go talk to Karen and decide for yourself, she'd said. *You shouldn't lose your virginity to some jerk you meet in a bar.*

Mandy was right. If she really wanted to lose her virginity, she needed to put herself out there.

She turned back to her list, making another note.

2: Call Karen at Military Match.

* * *

Lauren eyed her image again in the full-length mirror beside her dresser. A week had passed since she'd made the decision to call Karen at Military Match. Tonight was her first date. Turned out Mandy was right. Talking to Karen had all but made the decision to sign up easy. The woman had impressed her. Karen had a firm vision for her business, one with her clients' needs at heart.

Over the last week, as she'd waited for tonight to arrive, she'd also added a few more things to her list. She wanted to make out with a guy in public, and she wanted to get drunk. Just once. After all, wasn't that what college kids did? She hadn't, and she wanted to know what it felt like.

She'd also made a decision about tonight's date. She had every intention of checking off a few items from that list, and if she was doing this, then she was going all in. Tonight she was going to seduce her date. Have a hot fling for the first time in her life with a decent guy.

She'd need help, though. She hadn't a clue what to wear, and she was so nervous she couldn't stand herself. So she'd called Mandy and Steph for help. She'd planned her entire day so that she wouldn't have to worry later. She'd gone to the bakery extra early this morning to make certain all their orders were filled and the shop's shelves were packed. She'd left Lauren's Chocolates and Pastries an hour earlier than usual, so she'd have extra time to fret over what on earth to wear.

When she got home, Steph and Mandy waited on the porch, arms loaded. God bless her best friends.

Now, an hour later, Mandy had taken care of her hair and makeup. Steph had brought over the wardrobe. Mandy, at least, hadn't gone over the edge. She'd dolled up her usual perfunctory makeup and forced her to take her hair out of the ponytail she usually kept it in.

Steph, however, had gone completely crazy. Tonight's outfit was something Lauren wouldn't normally have been caught dead in. The zebra-striped blouse Steph had chosen lay open down to the button between her breasts. The V of the thin black sweater overtop was cut almost to her belly button. The black jeans at least she was comfortable with, but they were tighter than she would have preferred.

She turned to frown at Steph in the glass's reflection. "Are you sure this is the right look for tonight?"

"You're just lucky I decided to let you wear jeans and not that skirt I brought over." At Lauren's frown, Steph looked up, meeting her gaze in the mirror. "You want to get laid, right?"

"Yes, but..." Lauren eyed her reflection again. As a divorce attorney for a local firm, Steph was the more adventurous and confident of their trio. She had no qualms about wearing something formfitting and low cut, and she had the perfect hourglass figure to pull it off. Lauren, however, had always been tall and gangly and just this side of awkward. She'd *never* worn something so risqué.

"Uh-uh. No buts." Steph frowned in admonishment. "If you want to get laid, babe, you're going to have to leave behind your schoolmarm wardrobe. I still think you should've gone with that skirt instead of these jeans. Show a little cleavage and a little thigh and he'll be following you around like a lost puppy."

"We're just meeting for coffee. It's not like we're going to a club or anything. That skirt was way overdone." And too damn short for her tastes. "You realize I'm going to break my ankle in these heels, right?"

The heels *were* gorgeous, and they *did* make her legs look awesome. She *felt* sexy. Her and heels, though, had never gotten along well. More than likely she'd trip over the sidewalk and fall flat on her face. As usual.

"Well, you look smokin' hot." With one last small adjustment to the thick brown leather belt around Lauren's waist, Steph smiled in satisfaction. "You've got a great body, hon. You just need to learn how to show it off."

And that right there was the flaw in her little plan. She wasn't comfortable baring her assets to the world the way Steph was. She had too many memories of watching her mother get dressed for one of her dates. She eyed her reflection again and sighed. But wasn't stepping out of her comfort zone the whole idea of this?

Mandy appeared beside her in the mirror and looped an arm around her shoulders. "He won't know what hit him."

Knowing that, however, did nothing for the nauseated sensation swirling in her stomach. She had one too many memories of guys promising to call but never actually doing it. If she didn't hurl on her date's shoes or fall flat on her face, it would be a miracle.

* * *

Trent Lawson paced the sidewalk along the windows of the Starbucks. He scanned the street around him as he walked, his heart hammering from the vicinity of his throat. For the first time in almost twelve years he had a date.

This wasn't where he'd seen himself the day he married his now ex-wife. Wasn't where he'd seen himself when he'd come home eighteen months ago with his shoulder blown out, his leg in pieces, and his mind scattered to the wind, either. Hell, he still wasn't a hundred percent. He was still healing, still getting a handle on his PTSD, and his triggers were everywhere. Just last week the pop of a child's toy gun had sent him into a tailspin. He'd hit the ground before realizing it wasn't real. He still woke most nights covered in sweat from nightmares about the brutal things he'd seen overseas.

How the hell could he support someone emotionally when he was still drowning himself? But he missed the warm body beside him in bed at night. So here he was, standing in front of a coffee shop, divorced and waiting on a woman whose name and face he didn't know.

That was supposed to be *fun* part of the dating service he'd signed up with a month ago. He'd gotten the name of the place from one of the guys he worked with. Gabe Donovan and Marcus Denali co-owned the custom bike shop where he worked. Fellow SEALs, the guys had become his good friends since he started there six months ago. Who else but a fellow vet could possibly understand his aversion to large crowds and loud noises?

Gabe and Marcus had a firm business rule: they only hired vets. A month ago Gabe hired Mike. Mike was army, and his wife, Karen, owned the premier matchmaking service Military Match. Which was how he'd come to find himself here. Mike could talk the Pope into going to a strip joint and had convinced Trent to give Military Match a try.

When he'd woken in the hospital a year and a half ago, he'd promised himself he'd do everything the guys who died that day in the desert couldn't—he'd live his life. He wanted...Hell, he didn't even know. To date. To go out and have a little fun. Getting laid might be nice.

Everything he currently wasn't doing, which was why he'd signed up with Military Match. It went a long way that the place had a good reputation. They took care of the arrangements, and you simply showed up. And it was only coffee. Not drinks or a big, fancy dinner, so there was no pressure. It still meant he had a blind date, though.

He dragged a frustrated hand through his hair and turned to scan another direction. He was supposed to be keeping an eye out for a brunette wearing blue. The problem was, a dozen brunettes had passed him since he'd arrived ten minutes ago. On top of that, it being a spring evening in Seattle, it was barely fifty degrees out and, of course, drizzling. How was he supposed to see what she wore when everyone passing him all wore coats and hats? Unless his date showed up wearing a freakin' sign on her chest, he hadn't a clue how he'd recognize her.

She could be any one of the women seated at the café's outdoor tables.

Hell. He'd no doubt keel over before she ever got here.

He turned again to pace the other direction when a sight stopped him cold. Twenty feet away, a woman stood at the other end of the building. Hands tucked in the pockets of her black coat, she seemed to be waiting. Her head moved as if she scanned the crowd around her. Although he only had the back view of her, he'd long since learned to recognize the slender length of her body.

It was the curve of her tight little ass, however, that sealed the deal. He'd spent the last year trying not to notice how incredible that ass looked in a pair of worn jeans. Never mind that the ones she was wearing right now were fitted to her body, showcasing incredible curves.

Lauren Hayes. His heart hammered as his gaze zeroed in on the peacock-blue scarf peeking out from beneath the collar of her coat. Like a neon freakin' sign, it shouted at him.

Shit. If she was his date tonight, he was screwed. Lauren was his baby sister's best friend, not to mention she was ten years his junior. That made her strictly off-limits. He'd known her long enough to watch her go from a gawky preteen into a beautiful woman. He hadn't noticed exactly *how* beautiful until after he'd come home. After she'd spent hours at his place, cooking for him, helping him clean...and forcing him to get up and live.

God. What the hell would Mandy say if she found out he had the hots for her best friend? Hell, who was he kidding? She'd probably be happy he was at least dating someone. Not that he intended to give in to his attraction. She was still off-limits as far as he was concerned, which meant whatever he felt for her would be quashed.

Telling himself that didn't stop his gaze from caressing the curve of her ass again, though. Or his cock from leaping in his jeans, reminding him how long it had been since he'd last had sex. Not quite two years. He and Wendy had made love the night before his last deployment. Six months later he'd gotten her *Dear John* letter, telling him she'd fallen in love with someone else and she was leaving him. The price of being married to a Navy SEAL who was often gone for ten months at a time had been too high for her. He'd come home in pieces to divorce papers waiting for him.

He eyed Lauren again. Shit. He couldn't stand here all night gawking at her or he'd never find out whether she was his date or not.

He approached from behind and leaned his head over her shoulder. "Fancy meeting you here."

She started and whipped around to face him, eyes wide, but wobbled on her four-inch platform heels and pitched sideways. He grabbed her elbow to help steady her, and her hand caught the lapel of his jacket, gripping it tight. When she steadied herself, she let out a sigh of relief.

He chuckled and darted a glance at her shoes. "You're going to kill yourself in those things."

She furrowed her brow and swatted his arm, but the corners of her mouth twitched. "Because you scared the hell out of me."

"Sorry. Saw you standing over here and thought I'd come say hello." He let his gaze trail over her, taking her in from head to toe. "I was going to ask if you were just leaving the shop, but clearly you have a date. You look great."

Lauren was a button-down shirt and worn jeans kind of girl. He'd never seen in her anything quite so revealing. Her top hugged the contours of her slender shape, the low neckline teasing him with a view of her cleavage but not so much she spilled out of it. It was all he could do to keep his eyes on her face. That was more of Lauren than he'd ever seen.

"Thanks." She released his jacket and glanced down at herself. "I feel ridiculous in these heels. They're Mandy's, and she insisted they're sexy, but damned if I can walk in them."

He scanned the length of her legs, from the shoes up. "She's right. Those heels on you *are* sexy. That top is stunning."

Her gaze snapped to his, eyes wide and stunned. Yeah. He shouldn't have said that, but a soft flush rose in her cheeks, and her lashes fluttered as she diverted her gaze to the ground. A worthwhile reward for having said far more than he ought to. Lauren could be bold as brass when she wanted to be, but sometimes, like now, he caught sight of a more innocent side of her.

That softer side drew him like a bee to a bright yellow flower. That natural innocence made her shy, and he'd long wondered what it would take to bring down those walls. Who she was when she wasn't holding herself back. He'd bet his every last dollar that behind her shy facade lay the heart of a passionate woman.

He darted a glance around. "So, where's your date? He didn't stand you up, did he?"

The flush in her cheeks deepened, and she let out a heavy sigh. "I wouldn't know. He could be standing behind me, for all I know. I have a blind date. We're supposed to meet here, and I'm supposed to be looking for someone in blue."

His heart stuttered to a stop. Son of a bitch...

He tucked his shaking hands in his pockets and prayed, somehow, it was only a coincidence that they were in the same place at the same time...waiting on dates wearing blue. "Let me guess. You weren't given his name, only a vague description. You were told where and when to meet, and to wear something blue so he'd recognize you."

Her brow furrowed, those big brown eyes searching his in confusion. "How did you...?"

He swallowed a miserable groan. Fate was a cruel bitch. "And the woman who set you up, her name was Karen?"

Lauren's throat bobbed as she swallowed. "Yes...."

Of all the women to find himself set up with. Though he couldn't be sorry it was her. If he had to spend the evening with someone, it might as well be someone he was comfortable with. And he *was* comfortable with her. When he'd come home in pieces a year and a half ago, he'd wanted to be left the hell alone, to heal and deal with his shit on his own.

His mother and Mandy would have none of it. They'd insisted on caring for him, refusing to let him sit and wallow. Lauren had offered to help and had become part of the almost daily routine. She'd brought him meals, things she'd taken the time to make from scratch. Despite that he'd bitten her head off more than once, she'd sat with him. Sometimes she'd babble at him, filling him in about her day or complaining about the ceaseless rain. Sometimes she sat with him in silence, watching TV with him.

He couldn't pinpoint when exactly his feelings for her had

changed, but she'd become a friend. One he treasured. Just being near her soothed his ragged nerves.

All it meant was he had a date with the one person he shouldn't touch with a ten-foot barge pole. He wasn't sure he'd healed enough to handle everything that came with a relationship, and Lauren...deserved better.

Now he had to tell her he was the date she'd been waiting for, and he hadn't a damn clue how to break the news to her. So he stuck out a hand and winked. "Hi. Trent Lawson. I believe I'm your date."

About the Author

JM Stewart is a coffee and chocolate addict who lives in the Pacific Northwest with her husband, two sons, and two very spoiled dogs. She's a hopeless romantic who believes everybody should have their happily ever after and has been devouring romance novels for as long as she can remember. Writing them has become her obsession.

Learn more at:

AuthorJMStewart.com

Facebook.com/AuthorJMStewart

Twitter: @JMStewartWriter

You Might Also Like...

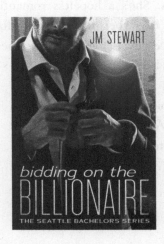

or her face. "He" is bikerboy357, the man who knows what Hannah likes, and wants her—every night—as much as she wants him. When he asks to meet, Hannah hesitates. But the temptation is too strong. And after one look into his sultry green eyes, there's no turning back.

Cade MacKenzie's never met a woman who wasn't blinded by his billion-dollar net worth, but "JustAGurl456" knows neither his face nor his name. Her words are so smart, sweet, and scorchingly sexy that Cade's willing to gamble she'll be just as amazing in person. And she is. But even as every delicious encounter makes Cade want Hannah more, what he wants most is her trust. It's something all his money can't buy. And now Cade will do anything to earn it...

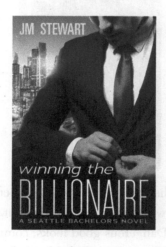

When it comes to love, this billionaire is all business...

Software mogul Christina McKenzie has loved billionaire Sebastian Blake since they were kids. So when Seattle's most famous bachelor—and perennial playboy—finally asks

Christina out, her fantasies kick into overdrive. Things become hot and heavy…but what's she supposed to do when she starts to fall for him? Sebastian's never been one to settle down, and Christina knows she's just another notch in his bedpost.

Sebastian knows that smart, kind Christina deserves better than him. But after the mind-blowing night they just shared, he's ready to turn a sexy fling into the real deal. Keeping his freedom is one thing, yet keeping Christina in his bed—and in his life—is all Sebastian can think about…

You know what they say: billionaires do it better…

Grayson Lockwood is every girl's fantasy. Fabulously wealthy? Check. Dangerous good looks, complete with a titillating tattoo on his rock-hard chest? Check. High-powered CEO? Check. Too bad none of that impressed the only woman he ever loved. Since she walked away from him three years ago, Grayson can't get her out of his mind. To win her back, he'll have to finally open up about the secrets he's been keeping. But first he may have to use a little deception.

Tired of her comatose love life, Madison O'Reilly spices things up by chatting online with a sexy stranger. All she's really looking for is a hot fling—and BookNerd seems flirtatious and surprisingly attuned to her needs. As their chats become steamier, she begins to wonder just how long she can hold out before she has the real thing. But when he steps out from behind his avatar, Grayson can only hope that Maddie will finally see his true heart...

Code Name: Love

Staff Sergeant Tyler Benson is a survivor. He doesn't give up on what he wants, and right now he wants Cassandra Stephanopolous. He thought about her every single day he was gone. Now that he's back, nothing will stop him from making her his. Plan of action: crash Seattle's biggest billionaire-bachelorette auction and make sure he comes out the highest bidder. If he wins a date with Cassie, she'll have to talk to him.

Three years. It's been three years since Cassie said good-bye to Tyler, and she's been trying to pick up the pieces ever since. Just as she's starting to feel ready to move on, he walks in, all cocky smiles and blue-collar charm. She's determined to keep her focus where it should be: on her thriving jewelry business. But as he lays siege to her heart, she wonders just how long her defenses will last . . .